Goddess

of the

Naples

a novel by

Colonel Mahmoud Iranpanah

Goddess of the Naples

Published by Wheatmark®
610 East Delano Street, Suite 104, Tucson, Arizona 85705 U.S.A.
www.wheatmark.com

ISBN: 978-1-60494-550-8
LCCN: 2010942711

Special thanks

To the following people
who contributed time and efforts to this book:

Jessie Wright - my son (Book Producer)
Ellie Oliver-Horist, my daughter (Book Editor)
Jessica Oliver, my granddaughter (Book Typing)
and Jennifer Grassl

Contents

1

New Beginning

New Orleans

I T WAS SEVEN O'CLOCK in the morning. The Spring rain last night, had refreshed the air. The clouds scudded across the face of sky.

Colonel Sean Taylor 53 years old, decided to stop to get a cup of coffee on the way to work: his command post, the Army headquarters in New Orleans, Louisiana.

He clutched his thin army jacket against himself, as he entered the coffee shop. It was a busy day for breakfast at the coffee shop.

Trying to get attention of a beautiful young lady behind the register. The nametag on her uniform showed "Angeline".

He smiled at her, and Angeline immediately smiled back at him. Like she does with all her walk-in customers.

"May I help you sir?" asked Angeline, focusing all her attentions on him, ignoring the other customers in the coffee shop.

"Yes please. May I have a regular cup of coffee to go Angeline?" Colonel asked.

"Sure Colonel" Answered Angeline, as she walked toward him.

She took his order, and immediately turned around to fill up his cup with dark, freshly brewed coffee. He noticed her beautiful body, as she turned around to give him back his order.

"Would you like cream and sugar?" she asked colonel, as she accepted his handsome smile.

"Yes please. Easy on the sugar Angeline," he responded. Noticing the delicate features on her face and body, he seem to like what he was seeing. Her beautiful white skins, dark brown hair, medium built body, and the curvature of her tiny waist impressed him. Her hair was carefully pulled back in a ponytail. His eyes began traveling up and down her body, as he noticed her beautiful long legs. Suddenly, Angeline turned around, and caught his eyes.

"Do you like what you see colonel?" she asked flirtatiously.

"Ahhhh! Yes indeed." Colonel was caught in action. He did not know how to respond to that.

"Your husband is the luckiest man on earth!" Colonel Taylor remarked, as he reached for his wallet. She looked at him with a smile and rang up his coffee.

"Why would you say that colonel? Are you married?" she said jokingly.

"No I'm not married. How about you Angeline?" Answered Colonel. Passing a five dollar bill across the register.

For a moment she was paused, then shook her head as she took the money.

"No, I'm not married either!" she answered, while returning the change.

"May I take you out to dinner tonight?" Sean asked.

"Tonight? I don't even know your name!" she answered.

"That's OK, it would be a nice way to get to know each other better. Please Angeline!" Sean persisted.

She looked directly into his eyes for a moment. There were thoughts circling in her head, not sure if she could trust him. Seeing her hesitation, he eagerly waited for her answer, but she stayed silent.

"Let me formally introduce myself then. My name is Sean Taylor. I was transferred here from Florida." Sean brook the silence.

"Well, now that you formally introduced yourself, it will be my pleasure to go out with you tonight!" Angeline responded with a beautiful smile on her face.

"That's great! May I pick you up at 7:30 p.m.?" Sean asked.

"Yes, this is my phone number and address." Angeline began writing her information down on a paper.

"I'm so looking forward to see you tonight. I believe in destiny. Do you Angeline?" Sean remarked.

"Yes, I do. See you tonight." Angeline responded, as she turned to help another customer.

"See you later! Hope you have a wonderful day." Sean responded, as he left the coffee shop.

Angeline's co-worker and friend approached her quickly.

"I saw you talking with that handsome colonel." Nina remarked.

"Yes, he is taking me out on a date tonight." Angeline responded happily.

"A date?" Nina asked.

"What 's wrong with that?" Angeline asked looking at Nina.

"Nothing, I'm just saying.!" Nina answered calmly.

"There is nothing wrong with going out to dinner with a good looking man!" Angeline said casually.

"Darling, men always want more from us. You know that!" Nina remarked.

"Nina! He is a nice man!" Angeline said in Sean's defense.

"I may be wrong, but you're my best friend, and I worry about you! Please be careful this time." Nina replied, as she turned around to leave.

"I will." Angeline said under her breath.

• • •

At 8:30am, Sean arrived to work. Sitting in his office, he was thinking about her, the entire day. There was something about her, that made him very anxious wanting the day to end quickly. She was vibrant, sincere, and her down-to-earth attitude made her very special. She certainly was different from other women that Sean had known and dated before.

Picking up the phone, Sean made a reservation in one of the most exotic French restaurant in town. He learned about the Chez Moi restaurant, from someone at his office. Regular customers who dined there often enjoyed the great ambiance, along with famous chef's cuisine. Sean wanted a special night with candle lights, and soft music playing in the background. There were a few fireplaces around the restaurant, made it look cozy and romantic. Sean reserved a table for two, near a fireplace.

It was 7:15pm. He was dressed in a handsome business suite, and had a single red rose in his hand. Driving toward Angeline's home, he found a parking spot in front of her apartment. He parked his car, and walked toward her front door, and rang the doorbell. After few seconds, the door opened up, and Angeline walked outside. Sean was speechless!

"Wow, you look beautiful tonight." Sean remarked.

"Thank you. You look very handsome yourself." Angeline said softly.

Sean handed her the rose, and she smiled at him. She put her arm around his, as they walked to the car.

Arriving at the restaurant, Angeline complimented Sean for his great choice in restaurant. They were directed to their reserved sitting. Upon seating, Sean ordered one of the best house wine bottles. Minutes later, the waitress brought the bottle, and the wine was purred in the glasses. Once alone, Sean made a toast. "To a new beginning." Angeline sipped a little bit and smiled. She was very cautious making conversation, and answering questions.

Sean sipped his wine, and looked directly into her eyes.

"Angeline, the main reason for this date is for us to get to know each other. It's necessary for us to open up to each other, and trust one another. This morning when I asked you out, I noticed you showed some hesitation. What was bothering you? Was it me, or something from your past that bothered you? I want you to trust me, and be open with me!" Sean said with all his honesty.

Angeline picked up her wine, and sipped a little. Drowned in her thoughts, it seemed like she was fighting deeply within herself. She shook her head and said, "No nothing about you bothered me! I just can't tell you…."

Sean held her hand, "Yes, you can tell me anything!" Sean said softly while stocking her hand.

Angeline lifted her head. At the corner of her eyes, a teardrop began to fall.

"Ok, I will tell you! It's a sad story." Angeline said quietly.

"I was born and raised in a poor family. I am the only child. My father worked in a coalmine, and my mom was a waitress. When I was thirteen years old, while listening to the radio, suddenly there was a breaking news. The announcer said," A few minutes ago, a big explosion at the coalmine, killed nine workers, and thirteen workers are trapped inside. A informed source, said that authorities are trying to save them." Unfortunately, my father died. After I finished school, one day I saw an newspaper article written by a reporter, about the Italian government allowing student exchange program. There was a scholarship given to a student to take classes in Rome. I applied to the program, and filled out the application. A few months later, I got an acceptance letter for the scholarship. My mom was so happy for me. She worked very hard to put me through school, but this program would pay for the cost of my education in Rome. I considered myself very lucky. I got my passport, and …"

Angeline could not continue speaking.
"I'm sorry." Angeline stopped with teary eyes.
"No, no! Please go on." Sean encouraged.

"Rome was warm as it was beautiful. I was very tired from the trip, and didn't sleep or eat, for couple of days. At the airport, I was carried with the crowd of people to the Customs and Immigration. After my passport was stamped, I began walking outside the airport. I took a bus into the city, and once I got off the bus, I was mesmerized. It was like I was in a dream-land. Suddenly, I heard a voice from behind me. "Are you an American?" I turned around, but didn't answer. It was a tall man with tanned skin, and warm blue eyes. He was very handsome.

"My name is Alex. Are you a tourist?" He said without hesi-tation.

"Yes, I'm an American, but I'm a student." Angeline respond-ed innocently.

"Do you have a place to stay the night? Would you like to stay with me?" I was too hungry and tired to argue. I didn't have any money or a place to stay. He took me to his apartment, and inside the elevator, he began to kiss me. It was hard for me to breath. No one had ever kissed me like that before. His hands worked magically, touching every corner of my body, as we reached his apartment.

"Let me get you something to eat." He said when we entered the apartment.

Few hours later, I woke up suddenly. It was middle of the night, when he undressed me, and I didn't resist!

Angeline stopped briefly, as the waitress came back to take their orders. They stayed quiet, after the waitress walked away. Sean thoughtfully drank his wine, and scratched his forehead. Trying not to let Angeline see any of his reaction. She closed her eyes for a moment, thinking if she did the right thing by letting her secret out.

The waitress came back with their orders. She placed the plates in front of them. Sean ordered another bottle of wine.

Angeline thought of Sean as a nice man, but wasn't sure what he thought of her now. Somehow, she felt calm and at peace with herself. She never told anyone about her story before, but he seemed tolerant, patient, and still interested to know more about her.

Sean wanted their conversation to go on. After some small conversation during dinnertime, he encouraged Angeline to continue with her story.

"What happened to the project that you went to Rome for?" Sean asked impatiently.

"Let me get to that later." She responded, looking at his face.

"OK then, I'm ready to hear the rest of the story." Sean helped Angeline along.

"The apartment belonged to Alex's uncle. One day, Alex told me that his uncle was coming back to Rome. He asked me to look for another place to go. My classes had just begun, and I didn't know where to go!"

"Alex took me to another girl's apartment. I began to live with her there. One afternoon after I came home, I found out that my period was late! I called Alex, but another man answered the phone. Quickly, I hung up the phone, and went to the apartment to find him. I waited for the elevator to come, but I was impatient! Quickly, I ran up the circular stairway to the apartment on the second floor. The door was unlocked, so I pushed it open. Suddenly, I heard a moan! I looked inside the bedroom, and found Alex naked on bed. Kneeling before him on the floor, it was his uncle sucking him! I couldn't believe what I saw that day, but It was a shock and I felt betrayed! I began to cry, while running down the stairs. I ran for so long, until a church appeared in front of me. That was a sign for me, to go into confession, and ask God for forgiveness. I lit up a candle on the way out of the church.

Early on, during my pregnancy, I tried to get an abortion. Climbing long and high steps to doctor's slim offices in Rome, was waist of time. The doctors acted, as if they didn't know what I was talking about! I was depressed and desperate, so I decided to kill myself. Once, I tried to throw myself over the bridge! An old couple passing by saw me. They begged me to stop, with their heavy Italian accent. Days later, I went back to my doctor's office, and he told me, "Don't worry about your baby, I'll find a good family and home to adopt your baby!" This was another shock . After I left my doctor's office, I went to library to do research. On the way back from library, I found a furnished room to rent. As my stomach grew bigger, it was more difficult for me to walk to my classes. So, I took a bus to and from home to my classes. The building had a maid to clean rooms. She helped me to learn how to speak Italian, and I thought her how to speak English. We practiced, while she cleaned and changed my bed's sheets.

The seasons changed. The summer, fall, and winter passed. One day, in early spring, when I was lying on my bed, I felt my water burst. Fortunately, the maid was there. She called my doctor, and we went to the hospital. The nuns attended to me in the delivery room.

"It's a girl!" The doctor announced. They took my baby, cleaned her up, and brought her back to me.

"The couples are here." Doctor said coldly.

"No, I'm not giving her up! I want to keep her!" I said while crying.

"How are you going to take care of her?" The doctor asked with concern.

"I will get a job. I want to raise her myself!" I answered without hesitation.

"These people can give her a good home, and everything that she needs." The doctor began shouting.

"No, she needs me. I love her." I shouted back.

"If you love her then let her go! That's best for her!" The doctor said as the couple came into the room.

"Is the mother intelligent?" The man asked, with concern.

"The baby has pretty eyes!" The woman said at loud.

"Get out of my room!" I shouted out loud.

"I can't give her up!" I repeated again.

"The longer you wait, the harder it gets!" The doctor responded.

"Here, sign these documents. You can't take care of her without any money." The doctor said, as he placed the papers in front of me.

."OK. I'll do it!" I cried holding the baby in my arms. Then I signed the documents, and they took my baby away.

Angeline cried hard, as she stopped her story mid way.

"I'm sorry Sean. I ruined a great date night." Said Angeline, while drying her eyes.

"No. Don't be sorry. I never expected to hear such a sad story. It's better if I take you home." Sean said with empathy.

As they left the restaurant, she put her hand around Sean's arm.

"I'm so sorry! I shouldn't have told you my life story, at our first date. Thanks for a great night. I don't blame you, if you don't wish to see me again!" She repeated again.

"I had a great time! If you don't mind, I love to see you again! Thanks for trusting, and opening up to me. One thing is for sure, we can't change the past, but we sure can change the future!"

• • •

Colonel Sean Taylor is a fifty-three years old man, medium built, tall, and icy blue eyes. He is a hard working man, and very efficient. He is a stickler for rules and regulation, and sometimes he came across as unfeeling and cold. He is the type of officer who sees the situations as black and white. He didn't care for people who broke the law, and didn't abide by rules.

A few days after their date together, one day the phone rang at his desk. He instantly picked up the receiver.

"Colonel Taylor speaking." Sean announced to the caller.

"Uh Angeline! I'm so glad that you called. I was thinking about you! This is a great surprise!" Sean said while talking on the phone.

" Are you inviting me to your place? Tonight? Sure, I'll be glad to come there. What time? Looking forward to see you!" He put down the receiver with a smile on his face.

Impatiently Angeline slammed the magazine down on the coffee table. She began to pace the floor, and looking at the clock. She was very nervous about her second date with Sean. This time, she wanted the night to be a very special night for them. Checking on the food, it smelled good and was ready. The table was set for dinner, and candles were lit around the room. Looking at her reflection in her mirror, she seemed to be happy, and satisfied about her appearance.

Suddenly, doorbell ringed. She walked to the door and opened it up. He was dressed in his charming uniform, and was standing there with a big smile. He was holding a big bouquet of flowers in his hand. She took the flowers with a big smile, and kissed him.

"I'm sorry about our dinner the other night, and wanted it to make it up to you." Angeline said with apology.

"That's not necessary. I have a simple philosophy, which has become a method, and a common practice for me. I choose to forget the past but learn from the experiences. I am not worried about tomorrow, since tomorrow hasn't come. So, with this method I suggest that you forget all the bad memories in the past, and look forward to a great future. Do you agree with me?" Sean asked when facing Angeline.

"Yes, I agree with you. Let's start a good night together, and make a new beginning!" Angeline remarked, when she sipped her wine.

"I'm starving! Whatever you cooked for dinner, smells great. What's for dinner?" Sean asked playfully. She took him by the hand, and directed him toward the dinner table, but didn't respond to his comment.

"I'm so impressed by your cozy apartment. After dinner, you must give me a tour of your apartment." Sean remarked, as he looked around.

"OK I promise. Dinner is ready now." She responded as she walked toward the kitchen.

She placed the dinner on the table, and sat next to him. He took her hand into his, and raised it slowly toward his lips. While looking at her, he gently gave it a soft kiss. It was like a dream. A rush of warmth came over her. She tried to keep her composure, and deny the desire to kiss him again.

As they finished dinner, his eyes never left Angeline's face. Her long hair drifted, in soft strands over her shoulders. He imagined what it would be like to stroke her creamy cheek with his finger tips, to kiss her at the base of her smooth long neck.

A few moments later, she was in his arms. He held her tight. His passionate kisses made her head slowly tilt from one side to other. He increased the intensity of his kisses on her neck and shoulders, before finding his way back to her lips again. She was hungry for his kisses, as each moment passed. They explored each other's body, by soft touches, and little tight compressions.

Suddenly, Sean picked her up, and carried her to the bedroom. He gently placed her on the bed, as he continued kissing and stroking her. He helped her undress, as she helped him take his shirt off. She put her hot feverish lips on his bear chest, giving him love bites all over. Now, he was standing above her, looking at her nude body on the bed. He caught the glimpse of their reflection, on the side full-length's mirror, across the wall. His passion rose, to a higher level.

Sean turned her over onto her stomach, and began kissing her back with intensity. She responded by loud moans, and great pleasure. He kissed her, like he has done to no other! She felt his passion raising, his erect penis was hard pressing against her body. It was making it unbearable to resist the temptation of making love to him. A desire filled them both, rising it to a ultimate satisfying climax.

"Angeline, listen to me! I fell in love with you the first moment that I saw you! More than anything else in the world, I need you to love me! I want you to be mine! I need you! Do you understand?" Sean whispered softly into her ears.

"What do you want from me?" She asked responding to his demand.

"I want you to marry me, and be my wife! I want to take care of you for the rest of our lives together!" Sean whispered carefully. He knew, she couldn't resist his kisses any more.

"Do you mean that Sean?" Angeline responded, with her eyes closed.

"You said that you believe in destiny like I do! I also believe in love at the first sight! I believe that you and me are made for each other! I don't want to live my life without you!" Sean expressed his thoughts with all his convection.

"Of course I do! I don't know!" Angeline responded in confusion.

He took her into his arms, held her, and pleaded with her.

Withholding sex from her until she responded positively to his demand.

"We need each other Angeline!" Sean whispered. She didn't get a chance to respond back to him, as he took her breath away with sheer passion, and excitement at that moment. She moaned at loud, "Uhhh!" She gasped for air again, ready for another satisfying moment. In sheer excitement, and satisfaction she yielded her body toward him. He placed his lips onto hers taking her passion higher. Now, she was begging him to make love to her! Her head fell back, exposing her soft throat in acceptance to his invitation to love making. He could feel her beating pulse against his heated lips. Her body was shaking with desire, and the nerves ending with a quiver. She wanted the ultimate satisfaction. "Make love to me Sean! I want you!" She whispered into his ear. Feeling the smoothness of his face against her own, the distinct hard pliancy of his lips, when he brought his mouth back to hers. She inhaled greedily of the clean, washed sent of this man. His hands were brushing against her waist, slipping down to hold her buttocks. He drew her even closer.

His voice whispered the words of desire again. That was the language of love, which she had never heard before. She leaned into him. Yielding to his passion. He raised one hand to touch her. With the other hand, he traced the curvature of her mouth. Slowly, he moved toward her breasts. He held the rich, warm swell of her breasts in his palms, feeling the thud of her heart. He dropped slowly to his knees, replacing his firm roundness of his hands, with hot strokes of his tongue. He could feel her hard nipples beneath his teasing fingertips. He heard her swift breathe, and smiled in satisfaction.

Slipping lower on her body, the softness of her belly invited his kisses. His tongue dipped into her thigh, searching for her most sensitive place. Her skin rippled against his mouth. The muscles of her body were contracting, as his thumb pressed hard against the sharp points of her hipbones. He heard her low moan of pleasure. She held his erect crown into the palm of her hand. Gently, he moved to press apart her thighs, to caress her with long strokes to taste the essence of her. He felt her shudder with joy, and fall limp against him.

Only then, she whispered his name. Sean…Sean... Her fingers busied themselves over his body, her mouth danced against his. Teasing him to new height of arousal, she put more kisses on his chest. Searching the flesh, as she uncovered it, he was aching with longing beyond the possibility of greater stimulation. Laying alongside of him, exploring, teasing, and pleasuring, as he had done for her. They discovered that there are no limits to their love making!

She kneeled up, and kissed his lips softly. He reached up, drawing her beneath him. He bent, and thrust deep within her, where he felt her body convulse in glory, and was lost in ultimate satisfaction and passion. She let out a loud groan of pleasure. Still locked together in the silence of the room, they lay next to each other for a long while.

"That was incredible Angeline! ... I had never been so inflamed!". Sean said playfully.

She reached up to touch his face... "It was the same for me ... I have never experienced anything like this in my whole life before!"

• • •

They continued seeing each other daily, drawing to each other more. Every evening after they made love, Sean had to drag himself out of bed to drive to his home. He needed a few hours of sleep. Their days passed, in a feverish dream, as they attended the usual round of meetings.

A few weeks later, when Sean went to dinner at Angeline's apartment, she was concerned about being late on her monthly cycle.

"I know, from the signs of my first pregnancy, that I may be pregnant!" She said unsure about his reaction.

"That's great!! We're going to have a baby!" He said excitedly.

Suddenly, Sean got up, and knelt before her on one knee. He held her hand into his, and smiled.

"My darling Angeline, you have made me so happy. My life is so exciting because of you. I'm glad that we have each other. Will you marry me?" Sean asked innocently. She gasped in astonishment at the man who kneeled before her. He waited patiently for her answer.

"Of course, I will marry you Sean! I love you." Angeline responded happily. They were both emotional when the tears of joy began to fall.

"I love you too. From the moment I met you, I knew we were destined to be together. Your love has changed me. I was never good at loving anyone, until I met you. I cannot explain how I feel, because I have never felt this way before!". Sean stood up, and embraced her.

● ● ●

The magnificent marriage ceremony took place at the officer's club. The next day, they flew to Jamaica Island to spend their honeymoon there. Two weeks later, they moved to a big house, inside the base.

In November of the following year, Angeline gave birth to a baby boy. They named him Gary, after his paternal grandfather. Gary was a happy little baby boy. He didn't cry much unless he was hungry, or if his diaper was wet. Angeline usually fed him, and Sean held him close to burp and fall to sleep. As his father, he developed a very strong bond with his son Gary.

As baby Gary began to grow up, Angeline felt closer to her son. Sean was away from home a lot, busy with his army responsibilities. She spent more time with Gary at home. Angeline did not believe in disciplining children at all, setting limitation and boundaries, were off limit in that household. As the time went by, baby Gary's behavior also changed. Seeing his parents disagree and fight over him. They argued about how spoiled he was, receiving new clothes and toys all the time.

Angeline was a great wife, warm, and very efficient toward everyone. Because of her husband's high rank position, they had a very comfortable life. She believed in simple life, and insisted on cooking, cleaning, and preparing food all by herself.

Raul was a servant, who worked for Colonel Taylor for a long time. He was deaf, and Sean trusted him. He was a driver, gardener, and did most of the home chores and services.

As Gary grew up, he attended kindergarten, then elementary

school. Mostly at school, he would often steal money and things, from other children in the classroom to get his parent's attention. Sometimes, he destroyed classroom equipments, and got into fight with classmates. A few times, Angeline was called to the school's principal office, to talk about Gary's behavior. Still, she refused to discipline Gary for his actions. Mostly, they went without any punishments, and she made excuses for his behavior. She never discussed Gary's bad behavior with her husband, because she was afraid that Sean would over react to them.

One weekend when Sean was staying home relaxing, caught Gary in their bedroom dressed up as woman, with make-up on his face. He gave Gary time out, as his disciplinary action to punish his action. Gary was asked to stay in his room, for the rest of the day. When the problems continued, Sean began to punish him by spanking on his bottom. Gary didn't like that. He said, "I hate you!" to his father punishing him. Angeline was upset, not knowing how to react to it.

· · ·

One day, when Gary was thirteen years old, his father Sean came home unexpectedly. He announced, that he was transferred to a new command post in Santa Barbra, California.

"Honey that's so great!" Angeline said happily.

"We have to look for a house in Santa Barbara. I know how difficult it is for you to travel with Gary. So, I decided to go there, and look for a suitable home for us." Sean said excitedly.

"Ok that's a good idea honey. I can pack up everything, and prepare them for the moving truck." Angeline said thoughtfully.

Two weeks later, Sean called from Santa Barbara. "Honey, I'm working with a local realtor. We have seen a lot of properties, but I didn't like any of them. How about a large house, with huge living room, and a basement? We can remodel it, with new paint color and carpeting, after the seller accepts our offer." Sean said with excitement.

A few days later, Sean called back, saying the contract was accepted, and the house was ready to close escrow in one week.

Both Angeline and Gary were very excited to see their new house in Santa Barbara. She said, "I love this house! It's so perfect for us!" Sean was happy that his wife approved of his choice. It was a brand new subdivision, and their house was the only one on their street. A newly built home, among a few other homes in the area.

The furniture was being moved inside the house, when Gary decided to check into a home in the neighborhood, where two boys and a dog were playing in front of their yard. He heard the boy's laughter, and wanted to meet them. Just like Gary, they were all teenagers.

"Hi, I have never seen you around here before!" Said one of the boys.

"Yeah, we're just moving into that big house." Gary informed, pointing out toward their house.

"What is your name?" The other boy asked.

"May name is Gary Taylor. What's yours?" Gary asked interested to make friends.

"I am Paul, and this is my younger brother Joe. This is our dog Barney." Paul introduced.

"Glad to meet you guys." Gary said happily.

Paul approached Gary. Something in his mannerism came across as hostile, but Gary didn't know why.

"What school do you go to?" Paul asked.

"I do not know yet." Gary answered.

"How old are you?" Paul asked

"Thirteen." Gary said without hesitation.

"Me too. We are the same age. My brother Joe is twelve." Paul answered.

The sun had started to go down in the west, when they said goodbye. Gary walked back home.

Angeline and Sean enjoyed entertaining friends at their house in the weekends. Making connections with friends, and Sean's co-officers were part of their happy times. On a few occasions, Gary quietly entered into the guest bedroom, and stole some of their personal items. There were some valuables from ladies purses, and a few items from men's coat pockets. Gary did that out of boredom, and sheer excitement. Under his bed, he kept a secret box. Inside the box he kept all his fascinating stolen items.

When summer was over, Angeline enrolled Gary in the same class as Paul. She hoped some of Paul's good behavior would rub off to him. One day after class, Gary was interested in watching the girl's volleyball game. Paul and Gary sat next to each other, and cheered for them. The competitor team had better players, and they seemed to be stronger than the home team. Paul was angered by the visitor team wining over the home team. After the game was over, Paul got up and signaled Gary to follow him. They passed the hallway, and with a special wire Paul opened the door. Inside the room was dark, but they could see the girls through a peep hole, from the other side of the wall. They were laughing, as they took their clothes off in the locker room.

"Get ready to see some naked girls!" Paul whispered.

"Can we see them showering?" Gary asked with excitement.

"Yah, come closer and look through this hole here!" Paul encouraged Gary, as he pointed out to a bright small hole into the wall. Gary could see the girls shower together. They teased each other and laughed at loud. At that moment, Gary felt a rush of excitement while stimulating himself, and reached orgasm.

• • •

The news of stolen personal items at Sean Taylor's home reached Angeline. She was extremely embarrassed, and was worried about Sean's reaction. Immediately, she went into Gary's bedroom.

"It's clear that you can't stop yourself from stealing. From now on, you are to stay in your bedroom, when we have guests in the house. You are not allowed to come out until they are gone!! Do you understand?" she told Gary firmly.

"Sure Mom I promise. I will not do that again!" He said innocently.

Gary continued stealing at every chance that he got. As the time went by, Angeline had no choice, but to lock her son's bedroom door, before the guests arrived, and unlock it when the party was over. She felt guilty, but was annoyed and bothered by her son's actions. She was concerned, that soon Sean would find out about it, and have a real bad reaction to Gary's behavior.

It was late December, when Sean and Angeline celebrated a

Christmas Eve's party at the home. All their friends, neighbors and co-worker of Sean were invited. One of Sean's friend mentioned that money was missing from his coat pocket, and a credit card from his wife's purse. Sean asked for exact item's description, and Angeline promised to check into them, and return the items if found.

After the party was over, Sean went directly to Gary's bedroom. He was surprised to find the door was locked! Angeline caught up with him there. "Where is the key to the door?" Sean asked his wife. She didn't answer but moved to open the door. "I want to have a privet conversation with Gary! Do not come in!" Sean said firmly, as he entered into the bedroom.

Angeline remained outside the door trying to listen in. Gary was in bed, pretending to sleep. Sean began searching Gary's closet, his desk, and finally under his bed. Unexpectedly, he found what he was looking for. It was Gary's treasure box! Curiously, he opened it, and found all the items stashed there. All personal items, money, credit cards, lipsticks, and other misc. items. He sat down on Gary's bed, completely in shock. Quickly, Gary sat up on his bed, knowing he was in trouble. His father gave him a chance to explain, but Gary denied stealing anything.

"Dad, I don't know where these items came from!" Gary said, with an innocent look on his face.

Sean didn't believe him, and began questioning him. Gary didn't want to admit to his guilt, and Sean lost his cool. Under his father's physical punishment, Gary finally admitted that he had stolen all the items over several years, and promised not to do it again.

As the time went by, Gary got involved with the wrong crowd, and kept up with his wrong doings. At age 18, he was heavily involved in drinking and taking drugs with his friends. Coming home drunk and high at all hours of morning. Soon, the news of vandalism and graffiti in the neighborhood reached Sean and Angeline. They were very disturbed by it, but kept their cool. Most parents thought, it was a phase in their children's life, but were fed up with it. The news of stolen items at Sean's house traveled fast at work, causing embarrassment for him. Most his friends asked Sean to step in, and do something, but Sean thought it was too late to discipline his son!

On a Saturday morning, while Sean was home relaxing on the living room couch, his son Gary arrived home drunk as usual. He yelled and screamed at his father, and pointed his finger directly at him. "I hate my family!"

"You are drunk again! What's wrong with you son?" Sean responded, as he sat up right on the couch.

Raul was in the kitchen fixing the dishwasher, when he turned around and saw Gary standing too close to his father.

"What's wrong with you father?" Gary asked, as he step closer.

"Go get yourself cleaned up! Why don't you sober up before dinner time?" Sean replied, as he tried to ignore his remark.

Gary resisted, his father's instruction, and stood there. Sean got up to help his son to his bedroom, but Gary took a swing at his father. He missed Sean's face by few inches. That action made Sean very angry. Quickly, he grabbed Gary's hand, and twisted it behind his back.

"We have had enough of this son! You need to be disciplined! I should have done this a long time ago! But I promise, that you will never forget this!" Sean said with frustration, as he walked his son toward the basement.

He motioned Raul to help open the basement's door. Raul opened it, and followed his boss down the stairs. Gary was shouting obscenities. When they reached the bottom of the stairs, Gary tried to run away. But his dad's firm grip on his hands, prevented him to move.

"What do you want from me? What are you going to do to me dad?" Gary asked, while challenging his father. His father didn't respond.

"Are you taking me to the torture chamber?" Gary asked again, while making fun of his father.

"Well, you just have to see, won't you?" Sean responded angrily.

Gary noticed a hidden room in the back of the wall. Raul turned on the light quickly. There was a table in the middle of the room, with leather cuffs attached to it. Not realizing what his father was talking about, he entered the room. Sean had known about this room for a long time, but had never been inside of it before. They walked toward the cross shaped table, and Sean dropped his son on the table. Gary tried to get up to run away, but he continued making more sarcastic remarks at his father. Sean pushed him back down on the table, on his stomach. Sean motioned Raul to tie up his hands and legs. Raul followed instructions, and when he was done, the table was brought to an upright position. Gary was laughing at the whole situation, and making fun of his dad. Sean grabbed a whip, and hit Gary across the back once. Raul picked up the other whip, and hit Gary again a second time.

"I love it, dad! Why don't you do it again?" Gary taunted his dad.

Sean hit him again a few more times, then stopped.

"I can't feel a thing, dad! You can't possibly hurt me!" Gary said to his father, as he lifted his head from the table.

Sean dropped the whip, and motioned Raul to remove the handcuffs. As he looked at Gary's back, Sean saw that Gary's shirt was soaked with blood. It was dripping onto the floor.

"I hate you dad! I will never forgive you!" Gary yelled at his father while crying with pain.

Sean went up the stairs, leading to the living room. Raul helped Gary onto his feet, and walked him up the stairs. When they stepped into the living room, Sean turned around to look at his son.

"I HATE YOU! GO TO HELL FATHER!" Gary screamed at his dad.

At that moment, Angeline entered into the house. She saw blood on the floor, then looked up at her son Gary, standing there with a bloody shirt.

"Oh my god, what have you done to him?" Angeline asked her husband ,in shock and disbelieve.

"He had it coming!" Sean replied, as he suddenly felt a chest pain and tightening. He raised his hand toward his chest. Looking at his wife, he fell onto the floor. Angeline rushed to his side and screamed, "NO!"

It was too late, by the time the ambulance arrived at the

Taylor's residence. Sean had a heart attack, and died immediately. Gary smiled, as he walked toward his bedroom. Angeline was in shock, and crying next to her husband's cold body.

• • •

After his father's death, Gary went back to college trying to start a new life. He received the news about his mother's passing, on the last year of his college before graduation. He didn't attend her funeral, although he was very close to her.

Gary graduated with a Bachelor's degree from University of Santa Barbara. He decided to transfer to UCLA to obtain his Master's Degree. He had always been interested in the study of human sexuality, as he experimented with his own sexual interests early on. The study and research of gay, lesbian, bisexual, and transgender was especially interesting to him. He wanted to develop, and experiment more on that subject. Therefore, sexology became the subject of his Master's degree.

Upon transfer to UCLA, he looked for an apartment nearby. After moving into his apartment, he choose his classes, and enrolled online. On the first day of his classes, he accidentally bumped into a young lady, causing her books scattered all over the ground.

"I'm so sorry, are you okay?" Gary asked with concern.

"That's OK. Are you enrolled in this class too?" she asked politely.

"My name is Gary Taylor", He said, as he helped her pick up her books.

"My name is Mary Fawset. We are late for the class!" She responded as he handed her the last book.

"You're right. Let's get in," Gary said hurriedly.

Searching quickly to look at two seats together, Mary guided the way.

"Follow me, I found two seats next to each other." Mary said excitedly.

After class was over, Gary acted very friendly. He didn't find her particularly sexy, but she was looking average. He was looking to find new friends at the university, so he decided to start with Mary.

Mary Fawset was a 21 years old young lady, with beautiful brown eyes, tan color skin, and around 125 pounds. She was brunet, and full of energy.

"I just moved here from Santa Barbara a couple of weeks ago." Gary explained to Mary after class.

"Oh, I was born and raised in East Coast States," Mary volunteered.

"I will be going to Santa Barbara this weekend to visit, and relax at home. Would you like to join me?" Gary asked curiously.

"Sure I'd love to! I've heard there is a lot of partying going on in Santa Barbara area. It would be fun if you show me around!" Mary said excitedly.

They said good-bye, and moved on to other classes.

Early Friday afternoon, Gary called Mary on her cell phone. They discussed plans to leave around 2:30 pm. Trying not to get stuck in the Friday afternoon freeway rush hour. Mary was receptive. She asked if they could have an afternoon snack on the way.

Gary picked her up around 2:15 pm, and soon their journey began. She was dressed in short shorts, and a white short sleeve shirt. Gary noticed the button-down shirt, with few buttons open at the top. It was exposing part of her beautiful breasts. Gary purchased a red convertible car a year ago. He looked very handsome driving the car around. Mary was flattered that Gary liked her, and was excited when he invited her to his place, in Santa Barbara.

It was a pleasant drive. The wind was blowing in their hair, and music playing loud on the radio. Mary felt great about the weekend, and was smiling a lot. Gary drove into a nice restaurant on the way, and parked the car. They ordered drinks, and had a good time. He talked about his house in Santa Barbara, as Mary drank wine. By the time, he drove away from the restaurant, Mary was feeling tipsy.

A couple of hours later, the car pulled up in front of his gated home. Gary opened the gate with his remote opener. The car entered and stopped in front of the door. Raul came outside to help with the luggage, while Gary helped Mary out of the car.

They walked inside as she was laughing and giggling. Gary helped her to the couch in the living room and sat her down.

"Would you like something to drink?" Gary asked politely.

"Sure. I'll have a glass of wine," Mary responded while still giggling.

"Let me show you around the house," Gary said, trying to be a good host.

"Just show me where your bedroom is! I want to be with you!" Mary responded as Gary handed her the wine. She sipped her wine, as Gary watched over her.

"Okay. I'm ready!" She laughed out loud, as she tried to get up from the couch.

She was too drunk to stand up and walk, so Gary tried to help her up. Feeling his face close to hers, she began kissing him. As he walked toward the bedroom, Gary didn't find Mary very responsive, so he took her downstairs to the basement instead. Raul sensed what Gary had in mind, as he went toward the basement floor, and turned on the lights. He waited at the bottom of the stairs, as Gary walked her down.

"Where are we going?" asked Mary, while having difficulty keeping her balance.

"To the basement!" Gary said excitedly.

"What are we going to do?" Mary asked, hanging on to Gary.

"Oh, we're going to play, and have a good time! You'll see!" Gary said while getting her inch by inch closer to the chamber. Raul lit up the candles around the room, and then helped Gary to bring her closer to the cross-shaped table. He laid her down flat on her stomach. She was facing down on the table. Raul stood waiting on the side. Gary began to strip off Mary's clothes, but left her underwear on. Mary's head was swinging from one side to another, while Gary tried to spread her legs in the bottom. He put the handcuffs on her wrists and ankles, and stood there watching her with enthusiasm. Now she was fully strapped to the table.

"What are you doing to me?" Mary asked with a concern in her voice, still feeling drunk.

"Isn't this what you came for?" asked Gary, fully in control.

"What kind of game are you playing?" Mary asked, not sure what was going on.

"You must wait! I will show you!" Gary said excitedly, as he undressed himself. He couldn't wait to start his game.

Gary signaled Raul to approach. Raul tied up his hands and legs with cuffs, to another table. Standing before him, Gary was totally naked strapped up right to one table, while Mary was strapped lying down on another table. Raul picked up a leather whip, and moved toward Mary while Gary watched. He whipped Mary's back a few times, but not very hard. The first stroke brought her back to reality. She gasped in pain and screamed.

"Uh …..Please don't! Let me go! Let me go!" Mary cried begging him to stop.

"Mary, be strong! Take the pain! Pain gives you pleasure!" Gary shouted, while Raul hit him repeatedly with the whip.

"No!!! I can't take it! I don't want it! Let me go! Get me out of here!!" Mary cried out begging Gary to make Raul stop. She passed out. The pain was too much for her.

Raul continued on lashing Gary's back. Gary didn't feel any pain. He found it exciting, and had a feeling of real pleasure while being beaten. He felt sexually aroused! Raul freed his hands and legs from the cuffs. There were evidence of the lashes on Gary's back, but he was not bleeding. Gary motioned Raul to leave the room, then walked over to Mary, and took off the leather straps from her hand and legs. He carried her to the bed placed at the corner of the room, then began kissing her. She came back to con-sciousness, but didn't say a word. With her head resting on the pillow, Gary gently stroked her hair back, exposing more of her face to the candle lights. He kissed her on the lips and body, making her forget the pain instantly. She began to respond to Gary's warm and affection, by wrapping her body around his. This was the moment that Gary had waited for. They began making love.

After they finished making love, she fell into a deep sleep. The next day, she woke up not remembering what had happened, during the night before. She felt snug and warm in his arms, as she began to feel the pain on her back. Her cheek was resting on his firm flesh. Her nude body was cradled, in a pair of steely arms.

She tried to open her eyes wider, but it was dark all around. Gary was laying down on his back naked. Her bare legs were tightened with some special bands under covers. A peek at the distance, told her that they weren't in a bedroom, but in a basement with some tortures' crossed tables.

She mentally cursed from the slow cadence of his breathing, and thought Gary was still asleep. The morning sun light was filtering into the basement, as she began to wake up.

Thinking back, when Mary was fifteen years old and in high school, she was aware that she wasn't beautiful, but thought she was seductive and attractive. Looking herself in the mirror, she possessed a beautiful body, and medium round breasts. Her parted pale lips seemed aching to be kissed, and boys in the school believed, she was ripe and ready.

• • •

Mary's dad, Fred Fawcet, had no ambition or dreams for himself or his family. He had a ordinary job in their hometown working for a company, but times were hard and people were being laid off from work. All he wanted was to keep his job, in order to keep food on his family's table. He made enough money to pay the rent, and house bills. Working over time, to have money to pay for heating, and to guard a giant's cold winter away from his home. There were little time for him to pay attention to his young beautiful wife, and children, but wished his kids to stay away from trouble.

She remembered her father getting home from work every day. He drank wine to relax, and later, he would take her mom by the hand to their bedroom to have sex with her. The walls were thin, and Mary could hear all the sounds, thumps, and the squeaks of their bedsprings. She often wondered what they were doing there. Later on, her mom would come out with no reaction on her face. Mary was confused about their relationship. As she grew up, she guessed that was how couples make love! Her mother seemed nervous mostly, and cry all the time. Her father used to say to her, "Stay away from boys and strangers!"

Mary remembered a trip with her father to another state to visit a uncle. After a couple of days of visit, her father returned home, but Mary had to stay there for few more days. One night, while lying in bed close to her two cousins, she suddenly heard a heavy breathing in the darkness. The girls were in deep sleep, as the man suddenly approached her. He put a hand on her mouth, and said to be quiet. Mary could smell the whiskey under his breath. It was her uncle! She was frightened, but didn't scream. He went on top of her, and raped her that night. It was horrible pain, and she had to endure it.

"If you tell anybody, I will kill you!" Her uncle whispered.

The next day she saw blood on her sheets. Mary was hurt badly.

"Uncle came into my bed last night, and raped me!" She told her aunt one time.

"You terrible child! How could you make up such story?" Her aunt said with anger.

"It wasn't my fault!" Mary said in confusion.

"Nothing happened! You are a dirty liar!" Her aunt replied.

"I'm not a liar!" Mary said innocently.

When she returned back home, she didn't tell her mother about what had happened. A few days later, her uncle died in a car accident, so she never talked about him, or went to his funeral.

Every night, she had awful nightmares. She would wake up middle of the night, but couldn't get back to sleep. One night, she woke up feeling sick and nauseous. She was confused, thinking it was a cold or a flu. She pulled herself out of the bed, and went to the bathroom with a lot of difficulty. Suddenly, her mom walked in, "Mary are you alright?" She asked with concern.

"I do not know mom!" Mary responded as she continued to vomit. It was a feeling she had, may be pregnant! She was over-whelmed with misery, and her eyes filled with tears. It would be devastating news for her mother to know she was pregnant. She would even blame it on her, so it was best not to talk about it.

"Mom, I think its food poisoning, but I'm better now! Why don't you get back to bed?" Mary asked quietly.

She stiffened and pulled away. Mary had succeeded in divert-ing her mother's attention. Tears came down her face, while she turned on the shower. Her naked body was plunge into the icy torrent of water, hoping that the shock would subdued her emotional outburst.

At her school, Mary was a skilled high dive champion. She often met with her teammates to warm up, then would do her routine high dive platform, and spring dive exercise. When climbing high to the 10-meter platform, she felt all eyes on her, while driving. She was a consistent diver, and her coach complemented her, by patting her on her shoulder. "Great job Mary." her coach would say, once she came out of the pool.

Unexpectedly, she felt heaviness inside her lower abdominal, when she came out of the water one time. As she dried herself with a towel, she pushed down on her stomach with a low pressure, trying to make it feel better. She felt like needle pain going through her spine, as a warm liquid mix with blood gushed out of her!

"Help!! Someone help me please!" She screamed out with urgency.

Mary didn't remember anything, until she opened her eyes. She was in a hospital room with her mom on her side. She was holding her hand while smiling at her.

"Don't worry honey. I'm here." her mother said kindly.

She could see her mother's tears, and the pain in her stomach seemed gone. Mary had a lump in her throat.

"Mama, oh, Mama ……" She cried out.

She couldn't continue talking. Instead, she closed her eyes, and tears came running down.

"I'm so sorry! I'm so ashamed, and wish that I could die!" Mary said painfully.

Meanwhile, the door opened and a woman walked in.

"You are very lucky child!" The woman said softly.

"I'm going to throw up." Mary said nervously.

"No, it only feels that way now! But you will be fine!" The woman in uniform assured her.

"I am going to check your stitches." She said, as they prepared for the examination.

"My name is Virginia Fox. I'm your doctor." She said politely.

The doctor pulled back the sheet cover. She looked over

Mary's stitches, and was happy with the results. She finished, and covered Mary back again.

"Dr. Fox … what happened to ….." Mary asked looking at her doctor.

"Oh sorry, about … the baby!! He was dead in your womb, and it was a hard surgery to take him out. I am very sorry!" Doctor Fox replied.

Mary cried at loud, not knowing to be glad or sad. She turned her face away, as tears were sliding down her cheeks. When doctor Fox left the room, Mary's mom entered. She sat next to her bed, and held on to her hand.

"Honey, I'm sorry you lost the baby. Why didn't you tell us about the pregnancy?" Her mom asked kindly.

"Mom this isn't a good time for me to tell you. When I come out of the hospital, I'll tell you the whole story. I'm very tired now, and want to sleep." Mary said nicely, before she turned her back on the bed.

A week later, Mary's mom picked her up from hospital. Mary explained everything that happened to her, on the way home, and they both cried together.

• • •

It was a hot summer day. Once they got home, the phone started ringing. Her mom picked up the phone, and suddenly she screamed at loud. Mary went to her side quickly, and saw her mom white as a ghost!

"Oh my God, he is dead!" She announced with a shock.

"Who was calling?" she asked in confusion.

"It was from his office. They took him to the hospital, but your father died from a heart attach!" Her mom replied in shock.

Early this morning, your father left to go to work. He was expecting a raise on his yearly salary.

"Did you tell him about …." Mary asked curiously.

"Yes, he knew about it and …." Her mother answered.

"Do you think it's possible, he had a heart attach from the news about me?" Mary said in a troubled voice, but her mother didn't say anything.

The funeral was two days later. She was having a nightmare every night. Her father's boss, and a few employees attended the funeral. Her mom appreciated it, and thank them on the way out. They brought a bouquet of roses, and placed them on the grave.

"Your husband was a great man, many people there admired him. There is something that I need to tell you, perhaps it will be some comfort to you!" The man said, as he came closer to them.

"Comfort?" Her mother asked in puzzle.

"We can talk about it another time if you like!" He replied, understanding the family was in mourning.

"Sure. Thanks for coming." Mary said politely.

After everyone left, Mary and her mom sat near the grave. They seemed to be at peace!

"Mom I have to tell you something! I've decided to study at UCLA!" Mary said calmly, while expecting to see her mom be happy for her.

"UCLA?" Her mom asked.

"Yes mom. I need to go away and start a new life for myself, I like to get my college degree from UCLA to land a good job later in my future. Please give me your blessing!" Mary said innocently.

"My dear child, I will not have you put your life on hold for me. Fortunately, I have both your aunts to support me. Your aunt Ellie is a famous movie star living in Beverly Hills!" Her mom explained happily.

"Mom really? Is Ellie your sister? My aunt?" Mary asked with excitement.

"Yes she is, but we are not very close." Her mom answered.

"Oh mom, I want to see her!" Mary said, as she was in a dreamland.

"I'm sure you will someday." she replied to her daughter.

"Mom, you mean that?" Mary responded hopefully.

"Let's go home now, we can talk about your plans later." Her mom responded, as she brushed away Mary's hair on her forehead.

• • •

Gary and Mary's friendship continued. Although, Gary wasn't in love with Mary, but he maintained their friendship purely on a sexual level. Gary finished his degree, and graduated with a Master's Degree from UCLA. He was happy and satisfied with his accomplishments.

On the day of his graduation ceremony, he felt alone for the first time. He wished, his parents were alive to see him obtain his degree. He watched other graduates with their families, as they posed for pictures. One particular girl and family grabbed his attention. Looking over his shoulder, he watched her stand by her parents ready to take a picture. She wanted all her family in the picture, but found no one to take it. At that moment, their eyes locked, and she walked quickly toward Gary.

"Would you please take a picture of us?" she asked with a smile.

"Sure," Gary said kindly.

"Right there please!" She asked while pointing out the place. She handed him the camera, and walked back to stand next to her family. She stood still for a moment while Gary took the picture. A second later, he handed her back the camera, and began to walk away.

"I will be glad to take your picture with your family!" She said at loud.

"No thanks. I don't have any family here." Gary said, when he turned around to face her.

"Oh...I'm so sorry," she said with a concern.

"My name is Sonya Routh." She introduced herself as she reached to shake Gary's hand.

"It's so nice to meet you Sonya. My name is Gary Taylor." Gary said shaking hands.

"What was your major, Sonya?" Gary asked interestedly.

"It was oncology. What was yours?" Sonya responded, feeling good about her newfound friend.

"Human sexology/psychology." he responded back.

"Wow....How did you get interested in that major?" Sonya inquired with a smile.

"Well, it's a long story. Your family seems to be waiting for you." Gary said as he watched her parents standing there in the background.

"Oh.... Don't worry about my family. They are happy to be here. We are going to have family luncheon together in a few minutes. Would you like to go with us?" Sonya asked him, with her down-to-earth attitude. She glanced back at her family waiting for her.

"Sure. I have no plans. It would be great to know you and your family," Gary said, not able to resist Sonya's invitation.

Walking toward her family, she introduced her parents to him.

"This is my father, Dr. Richard Routh, and my mother, Sandy," Sonya said smiling.

"This is Gary Taylor. We just met and I invited him to our luncheon," Sonya explained as she made the introduction.

Gary smiled and reached out to shake hands with both of them.

"It's so nice to meet you." Gary said, while looking at her parents.

While they began walking toward the nearby restaurant, Gary and Sonya tried to get to know each other a little more. Both parents were involved in laboratory, and cancer research. That's how Sonya found herself interested in the same field of work. Surprisingly, Sonya's family home and business were located close to Santa Barbara, very close to Gary's family home. During lunch, Gary talked about his family and expressed interest in obtaining his doctorate in sexology. Lunch was very relaxing and pleasant for all. After lunch, they exchanged phone numbers and information. Gary was impressed with Sonya's family.

During his drive home, Gary looked back at his eventful day with Sonya. Obviously, she was a very attractive girl, around 24 years old with shiny long beautiful blond hair, and blue eyes. She looked skinny but fit, and her body showed a touch of athleticism. A fair skin and a beautiful body curvature. She stood tall around 5-feet, 7 inches. Standing next to Gary, they were almost the same height. He could not exactly pin point how he was so attracted to her. It may have been, her honesty and down-to-earth attitude. She had a pure demeanor, which deep down inside, he wanted to change in her!

During their first year dating, Gary kept his sexual relationship with Mary, on the side. He didn't mentioned Sonya, anything about his friendship with Mary. He was sexually happy and quiet content with this arrangement. He always found ways to keep their sexual fantasy in the basement of his house in Santa Barbara. In fact, Mary kept his fantasy alive, and kept him going. There was a different relationship between Gary and Sonya. She was raised in a family who believed in no sexual relationship before marriage. So, Gary developed a pure love, and affection toward Sonya without any sexual gratification. They found other ways to keep their flame burning. Sonya insisted on having an exclusive relationship with Gary, so he broke off his friendship with Mary, and stop seeing her altogether.

Soon after, with the help of her parents, Sonya found a job in a privet cancer research center of a hospital and began working. Gary supported her decision. He made a decision to open his own privet office. With a help of a Realtor friend, he began searching for a small office.

His relationship with Sonya was great, but he was ready for the next stage of their life. He wanted to find a special time to propose. A very memorable marriage proposal, to the love of his life, would start a new life and beginning for both of them.

On a beautiful spring afternoon, he called Sonya at work.

"Honey, I have made a reservation in a beautiful, romantic restaurant at 7:30 p.m. today. Would you be ready?" Gary announced to Sonya excitedly.

"Sure honey! I will get off at 5:00 p.m. I have enough time to get ready before you pick me up." Sonya replied casually.

After Gary hung up, he took a diamond ring out of his desk drawer, it was special, because it belonged to his late mother. A two and half caret, pear shape diamond on a white gold band. "I wonder if this will fit Sonya's finger!" Gary thought to himself.

At 7:15 p.m. sharp, Gary pulled up in front of Sonya's house. She was wearing a sexy black dress. The front of the dress exposed her beautiful, full round breasts. She was wearing a diamond necklace, accessorizing her beautiful long neck. He greeted her with a kiss, complimented her on her beauty, and opened the car door. She thanked him, and sat in the car thinking how lucky she was to have Gary in her life.

They drove toward the restaurant. The headwaiter greeted them at the door. They followed the waiter to a very special romantic place by a window, over looking the pond. Gary couldn't hide his excitement. He ordered two martinis, and pulled his chair closer to Sonya. Taking her hand into his, he looked directly into her eyes. Suddenly, he went on one knee, and slowly began to express his feeling. He took the box out of his pants pocket, and took out the ring.

"Sonya you look beautiful tonight. In the past several months, you have made me the happiest man on earth. I want to share the rest of my life with you, and grow old with you. Would you marry me?" Gary asked Sonya tenderly.

"Yes! I know in my heart that you are the one for me. You are my soul mate, and best friend. I want to share the rest of my life with the man I love and adore. I love you." Sonya replied softly, with tears in her eyes.

Gary placed the ring on her finger, officially, they were engaged now. He sealed it with a warm kiss on her lips.

Everyone who witnessed their special moment together, began to clap their hands in support of the newly engaged couple.

"Let me call my parents and give them the great news!" Sonya said happily.

She picked up her cell phone, and dialed the number to her parent's house. Her mother picked up the phone.

"Mom, we just got engaged!" Sonya announced at once

"Oh honey, I'm so happy for you." Mother said honestly.

"You have to see the beautiful diamond ring that he gave me! It belonged to his mother, and it's very special to me!" Sonya said, while admiring the ring in the light.

"Congratulations honey! Your dad and I would love to celebrate this happy occasion with you soon." Her mother said, with so much excitement.

"Thanks, mom. We are going to Las Vegas to celebrate, with a privet airplane. Why don't you and dad join us there by the weekend?" Sonya replied, looking at Gary for a approval. Gary nodded.

"Sure honey, anything you like! It sounds like a great plan. I will reserve the same private airplane to fly us to Vegas this Friday," Her mother added.

"Fantastic. I'll have Gary make a room reservation for you and dad," Sonya replied to her mother.

The next day, Sonya called work, and asked for a couple of days off to celebrate her engagement. Gary's new office manager was able to postponed Gary's appointments until the following week. Now, everything seemed to be going as planned.

A private airplane was waiting for them, as Gary drove to the airport. The pilot walked down the stairs to greet them. He could see the couple so in love, and was excited to be able to fly them to Las Vegas.

They arrived at the Las Vegas airport, an hour later. After gathering their luggage, they took a cab over to their hotel. Gary checked in, and they were shown into their room. Sonya could not stop smiling; she hugged Gary, and gave him a passionate kiss. Suddenly, Sonya's cell phone rang! She looked at the caller ID but didn't recognize the number.

"Hello?" she answered hesitantly.

"Are you Sonya Routh?" The caller asked impatiently.

"May I ask who is calling?" Sonya asked with a concern.

"Yes, this is the police department. I'm Officer Mulkey. I have to inform you that there has been an accident involving your parents."

"What kind of accident?" Sonya asked, while holding Gary's hand.

"I'm sorry to inform you that your parents have been killed in a car accident, about an hour ago. We are investigating matters, but I'm sorry for your loss." Officer Mulkey explained.

"Are you sure? Sonya said, shaking uncontrollably. She dropped the phone, and lost consciousness.

"Hello? Hello? Miss Routh, are you still there?" The officer asked, but there was no answer.

• • •

Gary and Sonya were devastated upon hearing the news. They left the hotel at once to return back to Los Angeles. Gary tried to comfort Sonya on the way, but it didn't help. She continued crying uncontrollably. Upon arrival to LAX airport, Gary contacted Officer Mulkey. He tried to arrange a suitable time for them to identify the bodies. The police had determined a drunk driver caused the accident.

Sonya was being encouraged by Gary to spend more time at his house, but she simply refused wanting to stay at her house. She wanted to be alone, and deal with her sorrow. The following day, Gary returned to his office. He continued seeing new patients. In between his appointments, he coordinated the funeral for Sonya's parents. He informed Sonya's close family and friends, the funeral date and time.

Shortly after, Sonya returned back to work. It was depressing to stay home, and her work occupied more of her time. Her co-workers thought it was too soon for her to return, but she wanted to temporarily put her grievance aside. The memories of her recent conversation with her parents on the phone were making it difficult for her to concentrate. It was hard to focus on her new fiancé, and their life's journey together. Every time she looked at her new diamond engagement ring, on her finger, it reminded her of the great future waiting for them.

There were some changes within her office, they had hired new staff. The whole office was talking about a doctor named, Timothy Forist. People in the office, often talked about his gentle, kind personality, and demeanor. She wasn't sure what the fuss was about!

Timothy Forest was a tall handsome man, about thirty five years old. He was built solid, with blond hair, and blue eyes. He was athletically built, and educated at Harvard University with a MBA. Shortly after his graduation, he traveled to China to follow his passion. His dream was to find a cure for cancer. He conducted research and development on his theories.

One day, while Sonya was working in her office, Timothy stopped by to meet her. He offered his condolences. She didn't expect that, but thanked him for it.

After the funeral, things began to settle down more. Gary wanted Sonya to move in with him again, and set a date for their wedding. She agreed, but decided not to have a large wedding. She wanted to keep it simple, a court house wedding with a few friends attending. Gary agreed, and ten days later they got married happily. The Palm Springs was the destination of their honeymoon.

A beautiful honeymoon suite was reserved at a prestigious hotels, outside Palm Springs. They were so looking forward to a quiet romantic dinner, and champagne in the comfort of their room. Sonya felt like she was in heaven. A few drinks before dinner, had her tipsy and laughing out loud. Holding her glass of champagne, she began taking off her clothes one by one. She danced provocatively with a soft music in the background. She teased Gary with every move; building his interest up, to the moment they would make passionate love.

The beautiful Jacuzzi on the balcony of their suite was so inviting to her. The candlelight, warm water, and rose petals had set the mood for both of them. It was a promising night, full of romance, and love. She lowered herself into the Jacuzzi, begging Gary to join her. Gary moved to her side quickly, and began kissing her. Sonya was very responsive to Gary's touch, and went along with every move. While kissing her neck, he took her hands behind her back. She found it odd but exciting, in the heat of the moment. She gave into Gary's pleasurable movements. Quickly, he swept her up from the Jacuzzi, and took her toward the bed.

Sonya felt Gary's mood changing to a serious, very aggressive, and over powering manor. He reached for a soft rope beneath the chair, as he previously planted it. While seducing her with his kisses, he began tying off her hands above the bed.

"I promise you honey, that you will not forget this night! This will be a special night for us!" he whispered into her ear.

Her head was tilted back on the pillow, and she was enjoying the moment. With one quick move, he grabbed her legs, and tied them down with a rope. Sonya protested, but he wouldn't release her. This was just the beginning! Gary was warming up! This was his moment! He stepped back for a moment to take it all in. It was satisfying to him, seeing his wife's hands and feet tied up turned him on! Looking at her naked body struggling, she tried to free herself, that action made him even more excited. She started to cry, begging him to let her go! He ignored her. Approaching her body, he grabbed her hair, and pulled it back. That action hurt her more, and she cried harder. He placed a kiss on her lips, before he put a tape over her mouth to close it shut. He hit her repeatedly, with a leather whip, then proceeded to have sex with her against her will. He raped her repeatedly, until she passed out! It was like a game to Gary, and he loved it!

It was early in the morning, when he untied her hands and legs. He laid beside her, and fell asleep. She woke up a few hours later, badly hurt and bleeding. She quietly got up, and went to the bathroom.

"This wasn't what I anticipated to happen on my honeymoon night! What have I done? What kind of a monster did I marry?" She thought to herself. She had never been encounter with such vicious person, and didn't know how to cope with the dilemma. Under the shower, she began to cry even harder. What a unexpected and shocking situation, she was in! All kinds of thoughts began to flood into her head. She poured soap on her body, trying to wash away the pain. What do every girl want in their 1st night of honeymoon? A unforgettable night of passionate, soft, and romantic lovemaking! Instead, she encountered with a night of pain, rough sex, and a crazed maniac! Yes, this is a night that she would never forget! It was a nightmare!

The next day Sonya didn't speak to him at all. She stayed away, and kept to herself. There were mixture of sadness, disappointed, and feeling of being ashamed to have married him. Deep down inside, she thought Gary was acting up trying to dominate her. She had never seen him crazy like that before!

Around lunchtime, they met up at the hotel's restaurant. She said "I don't feel good, I want to go home!" Gary got up from his chair and said, "Honey, we are on our honeymoon!"

A few days later, they arrived home. Unpacking their suitcase in the bedroom, they tried to avoid each other. No word was exchanged between them at all.

It was another day at the office for Gary, but Sonya was drowned in her own thoughts at work. She remained quiet and focus on her work all day. She cried privately a few times, but tried to keep her composure when her co-worker were present.

Timothy sensed something was wrong, but continued working side-by her side, to build her confidence in him. She was unhappy with her life, but didn't want to talk about it with anyone.

A week later, Gary purchased a very expensive necklace for Sonya, to smooth things out a little. He ordered Raul to prepare a special dinner for them at home, in Santa Barbara. He poured a glass of wine for her, and pleasantly surprised her at the dinner table. She opened the gift with a smile.

"I love it! Thanks Honey!" she said with excitement.

"Anything for you dear," Gary said kindly.

"Can you put it on me?" Sonya asked happily.

"Sure, Honey." Gary responded affectionately.

After dinner they went to the master bedroom, to get ready for bed. Gary watched her undress. She put on a see-through black negligee, and slowly began to take off her jewelry. While sitting in front of her make-up table, she began to comb her hair. Gary was building up excitement, while lying on the bed watching her. He got up and went toward her.

Kneeling down on the floor, he kissed and hugged her. She was hungry for his kisses, and leaned more toward him by arching her back. He swept her off the chair, and walked toward the bed. Her eyes were closed trying to enjoy the moment. From the nightstand next to the bed, Gary managed to pull out the handcuffs with one hand, and with the other, he grabbed Sonya's hand. The sound of the handcuff clicking on her wrists brought her back to reality again! She opened her eyes. Gary was sitting on top of her body. She pleaded with him, but he ignored her! She resisted, by violently kicking him off the bed, then got up from bed, and walked backward toward the corner of the room. She sat on the floor next to the dresser. Gary like challenges, but he was angry with her action. He got up from the floor. His demeanor had changed into something evil, in such a short time! Quickly, he walked over to her, and slapped her face really hard. He was punishing her for resisting him! What he wanted was a obedient wife! She fought back, by kicking him in the stomach. In retaliation, he dragged her by the hair, and threw her out of the house. It was cold and she was naked! She begging him to let her in, but he had no intention to let her in at night!

The next day, Raul found her outside the front door. He helped her into the house, and took her to another bedroom. She sat down on a chair, and wrapped a warm blanket around herself. Leaving the room, he felt sorry for her. Quickly, she took a shower and got dressed to go to work.

• • •

It was 7 a.m. when she arrived at work. She went directly to her office, and closed the door. It was so early in the morning, and she assumed there was no one else in the office. When she entered into the kitchen, she was surprised to find a pot of freshly brewed coffee. A hot cup of coffee was exactly what she needed. Suddenly, she noticed Timothy was standing there, by the coffee machine waiting.

"Good morning, Sonya," Timothy said pleasantly.

"Good morning," she replied politely.

"May I get you a cup of coffee?" He asked, with a smile on his face.

"Yes, thank you." She smiled.

"Please call me Tim! Is everything okay?" He responded, looking at her face with concern.

"I'm okay Tim! Why do you ask?" Sonya responded, looking at him.

"I see some bruises on your face! In the past few days, I have seen you upset and crying! I would like to help, if you let me!" Tim said sincerely.

"Yes, It's my personal life!" Sonya answered hesitantly.

"Truly, I'm concerned with new bruises on your eyes! Is everything okay between you and your husband?" Tim said observantly.

"I don't like to talk about my personal life. I was very close to my parents. We used to talk about everything, when they were alive. Since they died in a car accident, I haven't been able to find anyone close to me to talk about my personal life!" Sonya explained.

"I understand. I hope we build enough trust between us, for you to feel comfortable talking about it! If you ever wish to vent out or talk about any problems, I'll be here for you!" Tim responded looking directly at her.

"Thanks Tim. I hope you keep our conversation confidential. My husband and I are going through some rough times, and we hope to resolve our problems soon." Sonya said uncomfortably.

She felt better after talking to Tim. They left the kitchen to get back to their lab, while holding their coffee cups.

A couple of weeks later, the relationship between Gary and Sonya stayed the same. They were cold toward one another, but courteous. Sonya slept in the guest bedroom, and left home early in the morning. She spent a lot of time working on her research with Tim. They went to lunch together, and Sonya seemed to be happier. They talked about their cancer research process, and shared their theories, and solutions together. Tim mentioned about a fund-raising party idea, to raise money for the cause.

Sonya felt nauseous one morning, when preparing to take her morning shower. She began throwing up, but her condition didn't seem to be the flu. She was suspicious of being pregnant. The last time she had sex with her husband, it was the night of their honeymoon. She decided to do a home pregnancy test that day. On the way to work, she purchased a pregnancy test kit. Upon arrival, she felt nauseous again. Tim saw her rushing to the ladies room. He followed her and stood outside the door waiting for her. She looked white as a ghost, when she came out of the bathroom.

"Are you okay?" Tim asked with concern.

"No, I'm feeling very nauseous!" Sonya answered.

"May be you are pregnant!" He commented on her health.

"Yes I just took a pregnancy test! I am pregnant! I'm sure my husband will be pleasantly surprised. I hope things would change for better, when he finds out that we're going to have a baby! He will be happy!" Sonya responded with hope.

She could not wait to get home to share the great news with her husband. Finally, it was 5:00pm when she made it home. Quickly, changing into a comfortable house clothes, she sat down in the living room. Gary was shocked to discover their fine china on the dining room table, and champagne in the glasses. The table was set for two, and he knew there must be a special news.

"Hi, Honey, how was your day?" Sonya asked pleasantly.

"It was fine. What's the special occasion?" Gary asked smiling.

"Why don't you come and sit down. Dinner is ready. I will tell you a little later!" Sonya replied happily.

"Well, it must be a great news!" Gary said excitedly.

Raul walked into the dinning room, placed the dinner in front of them and left. The couple remained quiet during dinner. Each one focused on their own thoughts, anticipating what the other had to say. Gary was hoping that Sonya had changed her mind, and come to her senses. He thought she would be more willing to get involved in his exotic sex ordeals. Sonya thought, after she gives him the news, his behavior toward her would change, and they will be happier. She wished with the arrival of their new baby, Gary would snap out of these rough sex cravings, and that his exotic fantasies would end.

They exchanged glances, and smiles during dinner. To relax more, they moved to the living room, and sat down on the couch. Sonya walked up to her husband, sat on his lap, and put her arms around him. Gary hugged her back.

"I have some great news to share with you, Honey!" Sonya said softly.

"What is it sweetie?" Gary asked impatiently.

"I am pregnant! We are going to have a baby honey!" Sonya said excitedly.

"What? I don't believe that! I don't want a baby! You have to get an abortion!" Gary said without any hesitation.

"What do you mean? I'm not going to get an abortion! I'm keeping my baby!" she stated without any reservation.

"You are going to do what I tell you to do! Do you understand?" Gary said angrily. He was trying to stay in control. Sonya began walking upstairs toward her bedroom. She was crying, and could not believe what just happened! Gary followed her upstairs. Once in the bedroom, he began shouting at her.

"You are going to get rid of this baby! Do you hear me?" he said angrily, insisting on an abortion.

"No, I will not do that! I'm leaving you!" she yelled, as she turned around walking down the stairs. It was too late, Gary was right behind her. He pushed her down the stairs, as she screamed out loud. She rolled all the way down, and dropped at the bottom of the stairs. She was bleeding hard and went unconscious.

• • •

Looking around the room, Sonya didn't recognized where she was.

"Where am I?" she asked the nurse.

"You are at Mercy Hospital dear," the nurse responded.

"What happened? Why am I here?" she demanded to know, though her voice was weak.

"I'm Dr. Robin. You were brought in this hospital, because you were involved in an accident. Your head has been bandaged due to some deep injuries, and your face some bruises," the doctor explained patiently.

"Is my baby okay?" Sonya asked fearfully.

"I'm so sorry. Your baby did not make it!" The doctor responded.

Sonya began to cry, moving her hand toward her bandaged face. The nurse rushed to her aid to calm her down. The doctor left the room upset with the unhappy news he had to deliver to his patient.

2

Sudden Death

FRIENDSHIPS LIKE MARRIAGES HAVE their myths: the myth of the easy and the difficult one, the active and the passive one, the needy and the self-sufficient one, the villain and the victim and so on. Sonya had to make a decision to go home and make peace with the man who abuses her, or decide to live her life as a single woman!

After her release from the hospital, she went to live in her parent's house. Parking her car outside on the driveway, it made her feel like she was visiting home. The flowers in the flowerbed bordering the walkway, were standing taller than she remembered seeing them. Feeling weak as she unlocked the front door. Every corner of the house, reminded her of deceased parents. She glanced at their picture on the wall, and put down her suitcase.

Sonya had lived a normal life. Great childhood memories, loving parents, and close circle of friends who always supported and surrounded her. She considered herself one of the lucky ones. Her marriage was a failure, but it was time to sort things out, and find a solution to a problematic marriage. She decided to contact an attorney friend to discuss her options. After she explained her situation, the attorney advised to file for divorce. "Leave you past behind, and move forward with your future." The attorney recommended free of charge.

During the separation and divorce process, Gary felt alone. He called Mary Fawcet, his old and dear friend! Just like the old times! Gary often wondered, why he hadn't treated Mary right in the past. After all, she was a nice woman, with a great sense of humor, who deeply cared about him. She was his best friend and confidant. She was ready to meet him again! Gary loved that about her, and asked her to move in with him. Gary remained friends with Sonya, after his divorce was finalized. It was time for Sonya to move on, and see what the future holds for her.

• • •

"Hello, Tim." Sonya said with a happy face, as she entered the office, one morning. She sat down calmly on her chair, with hands folded on her lap. Now, a single beautiful woman, with slender figure, with big mysterious brown eyes. Her soft golden-brown hair around her shoulder was partly clipped back with a barrette, leaving her neck bare and white. He felt good about seeing her. It was like the first time he had met her. He could tell from her behavior, whatever ill feeling she had before was over and behind her.

"Hi, Sonya! I'm so glad that you are back to work again!" Tim said sincerely.

"I don't know Tim…." Sonya replied nervously.

"I have some good news to share with you!" He said with a smile, as he approached her. She didn't show any reactions but waited.

"OK, as you probably know, I have been working on a special cancer research project, since I came back from China. I have made some progress, and would like to suggest that we continue working together from this point forward! Are you interested?" Tim asked, waiting for Sonya's reaction.

"Let me think about it?" Sonya responded teasingly.

As the days went by, their friendly relationship grew stronger and closer. They went out to lunch together, and spend a lot of time on their project at work.

"Tim, would you like to come for dinner, at my house sometimes?" she suggested casually.

"Sure!" Tim said promptly.

"It would be just the two of us…and we can talk…..," she continued.

"That sounds great." Tim replied casually.

" How about tomorrow night? Unless you have other plans…" Sonya asked, and then waited patiently for an answer. She was interested to know if Tim was dating anyone. He shook his head, and managed to bring a smile to his face, but didn't say anything.

"OK then, here is my address to my parents' house. " She said, already writing down on a piece of paper.

This was the first time that she was cooking for another person beside herself. It was a great time for her to get to know Tim better, outside the work place. Sonya was nervous. Tim arrived there, on time, with a large bottle of wine, and a bouquet of red roses. She greeted him at the door.

"Great place! Can I help you with anything?" Tim commented, ready to help in the kitchen.

"Thanks. I have everything under control." Sonya replied closing the front door.

"OK, then let me open the bottle of wine." He said, while walking toward the kitchen.

Sonya reached for the wine glasses from the cupboard. They both sipped the wine, and helped put food on the dinning room table. It was a pleasant dinner, and they talked about childhood memories, family and their life experiences. Their conversation was continued in the living room. They sat next to each other on the couch. Gary poured more wine, and made Sonya tipsy and giggly. Certainly, there was a great chemistry between them. Obviously, they were very comfortable with each other.

"I remember you telling me once, that you were an expert at hypnosis. Can you hypnotize me?" Sonya asked playfully, sipping her wine.

"Yes I am an expert at hypnosis. OK. Please lie down, and close your eyes." Tim responded.

"For the purposes of hypnosis, I need to borrow your necklace. Please follow my instructions carefully." Tim continued on, as he helped her lie down, and received the necklace.

"Please look at the necklace, and follow it's movement with your eyes. Your eyes are getting heavy now....." Tim started hypnosis.

"Now, you're getting into a deep sleep. Let's go back to your childhood life, tell me what you see." Tim guided Sonya's subconscious.

She talked about her childhood life, her parents, and how she met Gary, her ex-husband. Tim listened carefully, instructing her to go deeper into her life's specific moments.

"Can you tell me, the events taken place during your marriage?" Tim asked her, in a deep low voice.

She mentioned how she was raped, mistreated, and physically hurt. It was painful for her to remember her pregnancy, and how he pushed her down the flights of stairs, when they were arguing. She cried when she lost her baby in the hospital, and her divorce from her ex-husband.

It was time for Tim to end the hypnosis.

"When I count to ten, you will slowly come back to consciousness, and when I snap my finger you will wake up." Tim instructed her.

She sat up right. One look at Tim's trusting blue eyes, she was sure that everything was going to be OK.

"How do you feel?" Tim asked her kindly.

"I feel good. It's like taking a heavy load off my chest," Sonya said smiling at him.

Tim went toward her, and took her hands into his.

"Now, how do you feel?" He asked, but unsure of her response.

"I have to say that I have never met anyone like you!" She responded looking at his deep blue eyes.

He leaned forward and kissed her. His kiss was soft and gentle, just as what she had imagined it to be. Sonya kissed him back, wanting to take their relationship into another level. He held her in his arms, giving her a sense of love and security that she had never known.

The heat flared, and passion followed. Once inside the bedroom she reached for him. Framing his face, as their lips touched. He pulled her close while their bodies met. In seconds, they were caught in a compulsive expression of their need for each other. His hard lips ravaged her inner desire. Investing every stoke with his tongue. There in his hand, he swiftly and expertly undid the buttons of her dress. She felt his hand on her breast. Reaching up, she twined her arms about his neck. Her lips and tongue showed her hunger for his love. This was a clear signal, and invitation to engage in a night of pleasure, as her restless body was searching for more.

Her eyes were closed, as she arched her back. His lips traced her jaw, down to her throat, and the base, as she let her head fall back. It was hard to breath, and every moment was getting even harder for her. His hot breath bathed over her breasts, as she gasped. Her heart was beating fast, and she was filled with a burning desire. Her inside was wet, burning with delight, pleasure and passion for his touch. He sent pleasure through her body. Her hands had risen to grasp his head, and flagrantly while arching more beneath him, directed him to the center of her pleasure.

Minutes passed, as she savored the pleasures he lavished on her. He was pleasuring her, and that gave her the strength to observe, and touch him. She saw the hunger etched in his drawn features, sensed the quiver of his control, as his hands glided over her bare flesh. She reached up, drew him closer, and welcomed him inside her. She held on playing to his desire, in ways she'd never known or learn, it would captivate him. She found herself riding on a crest of passion. It swept her high, as she looked down watching him with passion, a force stronger than both of them. It was so powerful to fling them both into a state of mindless, dizzying, clawing need into intimacy. They reach to the height of their passion, where the glory waves were battered.

When the storm of passion retreated, Sonya caught her breath, and with one hand traced his face. It was glowing, as he gazed down at her. She saw the desire, and a need for words, but nothing came out of her mouth, except some tears. They were tears of joy, and he wiped her tears, and kissed her gently. "I love you Sonya!"

• • •

They continued working together, as their relationship went into a deeper level of love. The cancer project was successful, and rewarding for both of them, as Tim spent most of his time at Sonya's house.

One night, he walked into the bedroom with a grin on his face. She couldn't see what he had in his hand, hiding it behind his back. As he came closer, she searched his face for a clue. She didn't know what to expect! To her surprise, he knelt down on one knee, and brought his hand forward! He had a small box in his hand! There was a beautiful diamond ring inside of it, as he opened it slowly.

"My darling Sonya, in the past several months that we've been together, you have made me the happiest man on earth. I want to be with you as long as I live, and until death do us apart. Would you marry me?" Tim announced, as he sat next to her.

"Yes, Yes, Yes I love to marry you!" She replied with tears in her eyes. She jumped into his arms, and kissed him repeatedly.

• • •

A week later, while Gary was watching TV in his living room, he came across a medical interview. His curiosity got the best of him. The interview captured his interest. The interviewer was asking questions about the latest discovery of herbal medicine on cancer patients. Suddenly, the camera focused on Sonya.

"Can you please tell us more about your new discoveries? I'm sure you worked hard to find new solutions to this type of cancer," The interviewer said, holding a microphone in front of her.

"You are too kind, in giving me all the credit," she said modestly.

"Did you have an assistant helping you with your research?" The reporter asked curiously.

"Yes, in fact Dr. Timothy Forist and I partnered up on this

project. Our clinical research was done in China previously. The project has been very successful with our cancer patients," Sonya responded confidently, with a smile on her face.

"Judging from the smile on your face, do you have more than a friendship with Dr. Forist?" The reporter asked playfully.

"Yes, we are engaged, and plan on getting married soon!" Sonya replied proudly.

"Congratulations on the upcoming wedding doctor, and new discoveries. Sorry, we are out of time." The interviewer remarked, as the interview ended.

A few days later, Sonya got home from work a little stressed out. She decided to take a shower, and relax before her fiancé got home. Seeing her own reflection on the long bathroom mirrored door, made her curious to look at herself in the mirror closer. Standing there nude, she admired her curves, breasts, and long legs. They were her best features. She turned her back to the mirror, to see her round beautiful bottom. Water was still dripping onto the floor, but she was in no hurry to cover herself up with a towel. Turning again to face the mirror, she leaned closer to check out her face and skin. She brushed her hair, and applied body oil all over her skin. Starting with her neck, then onto her shoulders. She rubbed them on to her skin gently. Then, poured some more body oil on other parts of her body. Slowly, she began rubbing the oil onto her full, round breasts, stomach, hips, butt, legs and feet. She enjoyed taking her time doing that. It was relaxing, and had a calming effect on her. Towel draying her skin, to make it feel smoother.

Suddenly, her cell phone rang, bringing her back into reality. She always kept her cell phone near her, in case of emergency. She assumed it was Tim on the phone.

"Hi, honey, how are you doing?" Sonya answered playfully.

"I'm not Tim. This is Gary!" The caller replied impatiently.

She stood there frozen, not knowing what to say. Certainly, she didn't expect to receive a call from him.

"Oh…I didn't expect a call from you!" Sonya answered.

"How have you been?" Gary ignored her remark, and continued conversation. Sonya didn't answer.

"I called to congratulate you on the great interview a few days ago," Gary remarked, referring to the TV program.

"Oh yes thank you. Well, I have to go now!" Sonya remarked trying to quickly end the call.

"Yes, I heard you are getting married! You mentioned your fiancé, Dr. Forist?" Gary asked inquisitively.

"Yes! The wedding is tomorrow. I'm getting ready to leave soon. Why are you so interested in knowing about my personal life?" Sonya asked suspiciously.

"Well, we were married once! I care about you! I want to see you happy again. Where do I send your flowers? What's your address?" Gary responded, trying to keep Sonya at ease.

"No thanks! Flowers are not necessary. I'm pressed for time. I am leaving home for Los Angeles tonight at 9 p.m. So, if you'll excuse me, I must say goodbye!" Sonya said politely as she ended her conversation with her ex-husband.

The clock on her living room wall was showing 8:45 p.m. She quickly finished packing, and got dressed. Her beautiful wedding dress was hanging on the door of the hall closet. One look at her dress, and she could picture herself walking down the aisle to the man of her dreams.

She opened the car door, and placed her suitcase in the back seat. Her beautiful wedding dress was placed at the top of the suitcase. She got in the car, and slowly drove away from her house.

Passing along a few streets, before she got to the freeway, she was totally unaware of the parked cars nearby. Gary's car was parked a few hundred feet away from her house. He had lowered himself on the driver's seat, trying to hide from the view. He followed her car, knowing the direction she was taking on the freeway to Los Angeles. Surprisingly, the rush hour traffic was over; there was only normal traffic on the freeway that night. Gary's intention was to keep his car at close proximity to hers, so at the right time, he could put his plan into action!

A few minutes later, he drove faster, reducing his distance to Sonya's car. He was well aware that the road would be narrowing soon. A long bridge was ahead of them. The bridge was constructed on a high hill; one side near the mountain, on the other side, a cliff! Underneath the cliff, there were lots of trees and undeveloped land.

Within seconds, Gary got closer, and began bumping into Sonya's car. Trying to push her car off the road, as he tried to keep calm. Sonya was terrified, as he increased his speed, and pulled up alongside her car. Sonya turned her face to see the driver! To her surprise, she saw Gary's face! She was completely surprised, and very fearful of what he was doing. He put a grin on his face, when he rammed his car into the side of her car, running her off the bridge! She screamed as her car went off the bridge, then it was darkness, and her car was out of sight!

There were no witnesses. Quickly, he exited the freeway to turn his car around. Driving back on the road, he parked on the side of the road across from the accident, and waited. A few moments later, he started his car, turned on his music, and drove toward his Santa Barbara home, as if nothing had happened.

He parked his car inside the garage, and closed the garage door. A glance at his car damages showed scratches on the passenger side of the car. There were paint scraped off, from the front bumper, and was badly damaged. It appeared that Sonya's car paint embedded into his car! There was no way that he could drive that car to work, so it was best to cover it up with car cover to keep it off from unwanted attention! Clearly it indicated that he was in a car accident. It was time to buy another car! He turned off the lights in the garage, and walked away. Mary was watching TV in the living room, while waiting for him.

A few minutes after the car accident, a driver passing by noticed the iron rod safety on the road bumper was torn up on the bridge. There were fresh tire tracks going the same direction! Out of concern, he parked his car on the side of the road, to take a closer look. He walked toward the bridge, and used his flashlight. He was shocked to find a car fallen down below the bridge.

"Is anyone there? Are you hurt?" The man yelled out loud. He was concerned for the driver, and passengers in it. When he didn't hear anything back, he yelled out loud again.

"I'm calling 911 for help! Hang in there! Help is on the way!" The driver made sure he was yelling loud enough. Quickly, he gave his location, and the description of the vehicle to the 911 operator.

Within few minutes, a police helicopter arrived. The pilot landed in the bottom of the cliff in a clearing area. Cautiously with a flash light, he approached the car. Looking inside the car, he found a woman driver dead at the wheel of the car! There were no other passengers. The coroner arrived, and they worked to removed her body out of the car.

A few times during the night Tim had called Sonya's cell phone. Each time, her voice mail picked up the message. He was extremely worried, and walked impatiently across the floor waiting for her call or arrival.

It was around midnight, when he called her cell phone again. The phone rang over and over again, but went straight to her voicemail again. There were no answer at her home phone number either. Sitting on the couch waiting for her call, he fell asleep. It was around 5 a.m. when his phone rang.

"Honey, where have you been? I've been worried sick about you!" He answered, assuming it was his fiancé calling.

"Mr. Forist, this is the Sheriff's Department! Do you know a Sonya Routh?" The police asked calmly.

"Yes I do!" Tim replied in surprise.

"We are sorry to inform you that she has been in a car accident!" The sheriff deputy continued.

"Is she alright? Which hospital has she been taken to?" He asked the deputy impatiently.

"Sir, I'm sorry to say that she was killed in that accident!" The deputy informed.

"Oh……NO!" Tim replied as he put his hand on his forehead. He almost dropped the phone on the floor, shocked at hearing the news.

"We have taken her body to Mercy Hospital. It was a very bad accident. Her car went off the road on the bridge. We need you to make a positive identification of the body!" The deputy explained sadly.

"Okay, I will be there soon." He said in shock and disbelief, as he began to cry uncontrollably. Taking her picture off the nightstand, he began talking to her, as if she was standing there.

A positive identification was made, as it made it more unbearable for Tim to cope with her loss. A few days later, the Detective contacted him, and asked to stop by his office, at his earliest time. Upon arrival, the detective greeted him.

"Please follow me!" The detective said calmly, as they walked toward a police lab. Tim noticed many of the Crime Scene Investigative Specialists there busy investigating crime-related cases.

"Please notice this scratch on the side of the car! We have found another mark on the car, and paint color is different from her car!" The detective informed, while pointing out the driver's side, and the back bumper.

"Yes I see another paint color there! But what does it mean?" Tim asked in confusion.

"Based on our investigation, it appears that another car pushed Ms. Routh's car off the road on the bridge!" Detective Shepard stated.

"Are you saying that someone was trying to kill her?" Tim asked with a puzzled look on his face. He was more confused now than when he had first walked into the sheriff's station.

"That's exactly right! Someone wanted her dead!" the detective remarked quickly.

"Are there any witnesses or any report from anyone seeing the crime that night?" Tim asked in disbelief.

"No one has reported any incident! This is a homicide case now!" Detective Shepard said confidently.

"A Homicide?" Tim repeated in disbelief.

"Did Sonya have any enemies?" The detective asked.

"No not that I know of! This new discovery is shocking to me. Please let me know if I can help in any way to resolve the case!" Tim stated, as he was emotionally drained hearing the news.

3

Actress

PARIS WAS BEAUTIFUL IN the month of May. People in the streets stopped to watch a high school parade pass by. A week earlier, the Cancer Association invited Tim Forist to a seminar. A two-day seminar, which he accepted the invitation to attend. That was his opportunity to get away and travel a little. He was looking forward to follow up with the new discoveries of French doctors, on the effect of herbs on their cancer patients. He was happy with the results of the seminar, and upon completion, he caught a cab to the airport right away.

As he entered the airplane, he found his seat on the first class section. With the help of the stewardess, he put away his jacket, and made himself comfortable on his seat. Tim had changed his appearance a little, by growing a short beard.

The first-class seating was equipped with five rows of comfortable leather chairs. In front of him, there were variety of magazine and newspapers to choose from. He glanced at one of the magazine, as the passenger entered into the aircraft. He did not look up at the passengers, since he was deep in his thoughts about the seminar, and didn't notice a beautiful young brunette passed him by.

She was holding a little boy's hand, while walking to her seat. Once she found their seat, the luggage were placed under the seat as the little boy climbed onto his chair. They sat two rows behind Tim's seat. The little boy took the isle seat, and the mother sat on the window seat. She looked outside the airplane for a moment, and didn't notice her boy was off his seat. When Tim looked up, the little boy was standing next to him trying to get his attention.

Frantically, she got up from her seat and began calling her son's name. She couldn't see where he was.

"Marcello! Marcello!" she called out with a Italian accent.

"Here I am, mommy!" her son responded.

"Come back here!" she urged her son return back to his seat.

Listening to his mother, Marcello smiled at Tim and began walking back to his seat. The stewardess requested that all passengers fasten their seat belts; the airplane was ready for takeoff.

Outside the windows, the day was nearing its end. It was night time when the airplane left the runway. Once the captain turned off the seatbelt sign, the passengers were able to move about the cabin freely. Tim was looking at the beautiful city lights.

Near the back of the airplane, in the last row, a couple was seated. There was a black bag between them on the seat. Watching all the passengers carefully as they walked by. The couple seemed to be nervous and agitated, but they tried to keep their composure. For the second time, the stewardess asked them to put the bag in the overhead compartment, but they refused. They talked in a foreign language, ignoring the stewardess.

Thirty minutes after the take off, the stewardess prepared to serve the passengers with drinks and snacks. Marcello took off the seatbelt, and found his way to Tim's seat again. Tim noticed him and began talking. At that moment, Marcello's mom caught up to him. She took Marcello's hand ready to return to their seat.

"I'm so sorry! I apologize for any disturbance my son may have caused you," she said sincerely in her thick Italian-English accent.

"No problem," Tim responded with a smile.

The dinner was served for the first class passengers. Marcello fell asleep very fast, right after dinner. His mother began looking through a magazine to pass some time and relax. She glanced at the pages quickly, but her thoughts were occupied with where she came from, and where she was planning on going in her future.

• • •

The most famous international director and producer in the movie industry of Italy was Philipo Rousliny. He was a famous man, who was a legend in the movie industry. His only daughter Gina was Miss Italy. Later she became an actress, and lived in the city of Naples with her famous and rich father. Gina's beauty was the people's talk at Naples. She was built very delicate. In her teens, she fell in love with a handsome Italian man who worked as a comedian. He didn't make much money, nor was he famous in the field of stand up comedy. Against her father's warning, Gina married him. After Gina got pregnant, she asked her father, Philipo Rousliny, to give her husband a small part in one of his movies. But her father refused, because he didn't like him. After Gina's miscarriage the first year, finally she gave birth to a beautiful baby girl named Oriana. Gina went back to movies, and made lots of money. While her husband was bewildered and drunk, trying to keep his distance from Gina and his child mostly.

I was that baby girl! My mother and I visited my grandpa Rousliny every weekend. As I grew up, my father kept drinking and eventually he fell into a deep depression and illness. He didn't have any desire to see me or spend time with me.

During my time going to elementary school and high school, I went to a special acting class at my grandpa's studio. Everyone said my beauty was like my mother, but my tall and slender body, resembled my father. Most people remarked my body looked like Sofia Loren, with large beautiful brown eyes, and brown/blondish hair color.

When I was seventeen, during my senior year in high school, I was selected for the Miss Italy Pageant. I was one of the few girls who was hand picked to be in the pageants. The pageant judges remarked, "I was perfect to win the competition." Deep down inside, I knew that I was created to be a movie star! My features resembled my mother's with perfect skin, great legs, full lips, wide eyes, and perfect curves.

My father got lung cancer and died in the hospital. It was shortly after I turned 18. The last time I saw him, he was in his coffin. He was only fifty years old, but his thick white hair, heavy eyebrows, and wrinkled face made him look older than his actual age.

After my father's death, Grandpa traveled to Hollywood but asked my mother and I to move into his mansion at Naples. Weeks later, when grandpa came back, he asked my mom to take me to the studio for a movie screen testing. It was a new movie that he was directing, and he needed a new face for the film.

"Don't worry dad, Oriana can do it! She is very talented and comfortable in front of the camera." Mother Gina said to her father.

"You are right Gina. Oriana would be perfect for this film." He responded.

The movie screen test went well, and the verdict was in.

"Looks like you got the part darling!" Grandpa announced with excitement.

"Are you kidding Grandpa?" I asked with tears in my eyes.

"No darling. We'll start filming in one week. You are a goddess in Italy!" Grandpa Rousliny responded to his grand-daughter Oriana.

By the time Oriana finished filming her third major movie, there were no other film for her staring role. There were some small parts in TV commercials which she was not interested to do. She was frustrated but had to wait for another suitable movie role.

As her nineteenth birthday approached, she decided to have a little fun. Watching TV soccer games were fun and exciting. The sounds of people cheering, and encouraging soccer players to do better, seemed wonderful to her. A VIP ticket arrived in mail one day, inviting her to watch the soccer game live in the stadium.

Excited about the game, she arrived to the Soccer Stadium one hour before. There was a handsome young man seated there. Soon, he began making conversation about the soccer team, and the players. Their interactions were enjoyable, and the talk about individual players continued on. He talked about the after party, where a famous local sport celebrity was planning a party, for the finale soccer match in Naples. Most famous Italian movie stars were invited. He believed most people from Italy believed their team would beat Spain's team, and were eager to see Spain gets defeated.

The young man's name was Carlo Lombardy. He was a international race car driver. He knew Oriana's nickname, "Naples Goddess!" He didn't expected to see her there, and was in awe seating next to her in person. What a beautiful girl! She was delighted to take a picture with him, and sign a autograph for him.

Suddenly, the Italy soccer team entered the stadium. People went crazy, as each player's name was announced. Then, it was the Spain's team to enter the field. "Ladies and gentlemen, I have been informed that we have a special spectator with us today! Most Italians have seen her in the movies, and TV commercials. She is our famous, the Naples goddess, Oriana Rousliny." The broadcaster announced on the stadium speaker.

The Italian people were excited to hear that news. They gave her a standing ovation. She was the pride and the joy of Italy. That was unexpected for Oriana, but she enjoyed every minute of it. The TV cameras focused on the VIP box. She stood up and waived, blowing kisses to spectators cheering up for her. She sat back down, and minutes later the game began.

With each moment passing, the struggle to win the game for both teams were important. The first forty-five minutes of the game finished without any result. Carlo found opportunities to keep talking with Oriana about his car racing experiences, family, and where he lived. She smiled, when he told her about being single and was waiting for the right person to come into his life. He talked about his parents who were separated, and his passion for his race car driving and traveling.

"I bet you that Spain soccer team will win today!" Carlo said playfully.

"OK, how much do you want to bet?" Oriana responded with a smile.

"The loser pays for tonight's dinner." Carlo said, getting ready to shake her hand.

"I accept. You better get ready to pay for dinner tonight!" Oriana said taking his challenge.

The second half of the game made both of them to focus more on the players. Suddenly, Spain team took a shot at Italy's team. It was the first goal! The stadium went into a shock. Everyone was quiet when they replayed the game on the TV monitor. Only Carlo joyfully got up to embrace Oriana, still in shock.

The Italy's team coach asked for timeout. He pepped talk his players to be more aggressive to attack! It worked well. A few minutes later, the Italy's player took a shot, and it was the first goal for Italy. The stadium went wild. People did their dance of joy. Oriana jumped up laughing in disbelief. The Italy's coach put more pressure on his team one more time. Within few minutes of the first goal, Italy scored their second! The spectators stood up cheering again, shouting "Italy....Italy". The game ended. Italy won the soccer match and become the European Soccer Champions. People of Naples were pleased with the result. There were singing and dancing in the streets. Carlo got up from his seat went toward Oriana.

"It was a great game, you won the bit fair and square! I'm glad that Italy won. Looks like I have to pay my debt by taking you out to dinner!" Carlo said with a grin on his face.

"What bet? It was just for fun..." Oriana answered.

"No, no. I am serious Miss Oriana! A bet is a bet, and the loser has to pay," Carlo said humbly.

"Okay, Carlo. I'll think about it." Oriana replied.

"How about tonight?" Carlo suggested, then waited for an answer.

"Sure why not!" She said while walking out of the VIP box.

"Great! I know a nice quiet and classy place! We can talk and have a little more privacy." Carlo said, as he guided her toward his limousine.

Clearly, there was a attraction between the two of them while driving to the restaurant. Carlo Lombardy had a great characteristic features. He seemed charming, athletically built, high forehead, brown hair, brown eyes, and very intelligent. From the first moment that they met, he instantly had an effect on her. Oriana didn't care Carlo being six years older than her, as long as there was chemistry between them.

She liked the very romantic and classy restaurant by the lake. Their table was next to the window, overlooking the small water fall. Carlo ordered wine, and they talked for hours. Carlo was a very sexy man, and had a great sense of humor. It was a great tasting dinner. Oriana wasn't used to drinking wine so much. Now drunk, she was giggling and having fun. They kissed during and after dinner, and he reserved a room at the hotel.

He played her young body like a musical instrument. Embracing her into his arms, and showered her with kisses. Carlo unleashed his passion, like she had never known one like it. He took off her top, leaving her to take off the rest of her clothes while he watched.

"I have never been with anyone else before Carlo! I'm still a virgin! I'm afraid to…"She said, while standing in the middle of the room drunk.

"What are you afraid of?" He asked gently.

"I don't know!" She tried to make sense out of her words.

"Don't be afraid. This will be a special night for us!" He persuaded her to go on. He kissed her more to make her forget the reality.

Carlo was a very gentle man. He touched her tenderly, and with his passionate kisses on her neck, shoulder, breasts, and nipples to awakened all her urges to comply. For a quick moment he walked away from her, and sat down on a chair watching her. Provocatively, she took her short skirt off. It fell down to her ankles. Then, she stood standing there in front of him, with her sexy bra and underwear. Carlo stayed motionless. He anticipated seeing her standing there naked. Suddenly, she took her hand behind to unhooked her bra. It took a few seconds, before the bra fell onto the floor. Carlo was so turned on watching her perfect breasts. Moving her hip slowly, her hands slide down to her side next to her underwear. Slowly, she pushed it down on her thighs exposing herself. The dim lights from behind, exaggerated her beautiful naked body. This was beyond Carlo's dreams! What a angelic beauty! He wanted to explore her, and give her all the pleasures that she deserved.

It was like he was in a car race. Starting his engine, pumping on the gas pedal, drive the car as fast as he could. Walking toward her, he was building more excitement, and couldn't wait for another moment! He carried her to bed slowly and placed her on the bed. It was time for his clothes to come off. Letting his magic fingers do their wonders, with one hand, he pushed a part her legs, and with the other, he cupped her breast and let his tongue run through her skin. She was filled with pleasure. She moaned loudly as he intensified his touch. Then it happened! A sharp pain tore up something inside of her! She screamed in pain! He stopped for a moment, and then moved more gently inside of her. She felt a warm sensation, like warm water exiting out, between her thighs. She focused more on her lovemaking, feeling her body as one with him. Carlo began pumping his hips, making her reach orgasm. She gave one long, gagging moan and shuddered to a halt. She trembled with pleasure, like a volcanic eruption with little aftershocks that followed moments later.

"Are you okay? Did I hurt you?" Carlo whispered in her ear softly.

"No, I'm not hurt, but I think I'm bleeding," She whispered in confusion.

Carlo held her tight.

"I know sweetheart. You really are something!" Carlo said affectionately.

As the time went by, she was disappointed not to be able to spend time together. Occasionally, they met up when he wasn't racing, but mostly they talked on the phone.

Her grandpa arranged for her to look over some movie script, so she went by the studio to visit him and his secretary, Loretta.

A few weeks after they went out, Carlo called her on the

phone one day. "Honey, in a couple of days I'm scheduled to go to Rome, then back to Monte Carlo Grand Prix. I promise, when I return back we'll get married. Would you like that?"

"Carlo, are you serious?" She said in disbelief.

"Sure sweetheart. I love you." Carlo said honestly.

"I'm not sure if my mom and grandpa would approve!" She said in anguish.

"It's your..." Carlo said interrupting what she was about to say.

"Yes, yes, of course. I didn't mean that..." She said trying to explain.

"Oriana sweetheart, would you marry me?" Carlo asked again.

"I think it's best we talk about it after you come back from your trip. Is that OK Carlo?" Oriana said dodging his question.

"Ok, Chow sweetheart. I love you." Carlo responded with excitement.

A few weeks later, while Oriana went to take a shower, suddenly she felt her body ach. She walked out of the shower, and began vomiting. She yelled at loud to her mother.

"Mom, please call a doctor." Oriana said feeling awful.

"No sweetheart that's not necessary! I see from your symptoms, that you are pregnant!" Her mother, Gina said while helping her to lie on her bed. She was quiet for a moment, when Gina sat next to her.

"Mommy, are you sure I'm pregnant?" Oriana asked with concern.

"Yes, I am sure sweetheart. I know that based on my own experience, but will have the doctor do his testing later. Who is the father?" Gina asked calmly.

"I can't answer you now! But trust me mom, he is a good man. We love each other, and I'm happy to have his baby. Please don't say anything to anyone, especially grandpa! Promise me!" Oriana asked her mom for secrecy.

"Ok sweetie. Stay in bed today. Don't come to the studio. When was your last period?" Gina asked pryingly.

"Over a month ago." Oriana responded to her mom.

"OK just to be sure, I'll get a pregnancy test from the

pharmacy this afternoon." Her mom responded taking charge of the situation.

After Gina left the room, Oriana closed her eyes. There were teardrops sliding down from the corner of her eyes onto her cheeks. The truth was, that she didn't know anything about Carlo. Who was he? What was his background? Who were his family members? She thought to herself. "What have I done? What if he is married and has children." Bad thoughts went through her mind and tormented her. It mocked her, with a fierce yearning, that the baby growing inside of her, would look like Carlo Lombardy!

She laced her fingers over the hard mound of her belly. This sign was the beginning of her future pains. She should've dated Carlo longer, before they had sex. It was too late now and she was pregnant!

"Oh God please help me". Oriana said helplessly.

Gina had the pregnancy test kit when she returned home. The mother and daughter work together to find out if the test result was positive for her pregnancy. They both cried when the test came positive! One week passed, and there were no calls from Carlo Lombardy. She was upset and angry with him not calling. Yet, she couldn't bring herself to call him.

Eight months passed, as she got closer to delivery of her baby. Sometimes she woke up middle of the night and lie on her bed sleepless for hours thinking about Carlo. She didn't want to let negative thought ruin her days. One day, after she woke up and took her shower she felt good. After her breakfast with her mom Gina, her home phone rang.

"Hello?" Who? You want to talk to Oriana? Just a minute!" Her mother Gina said when she picked up the phone.

"Somebody wants to talk to you! " Gina said, as she tried to hand over the phone.

"Hello Carlo? Is it you? Why didn't you call me? Where have you been? What do you mean? You have wife and kids? What?!!" Oriana asked in confusion.

"I am sorry Oriana not to call you. I'm ashamed that I deceived you. I couldn't tell the truth. I don't know how to fix the problem. Please forgive me! I'm going to be in a race in just a few minutes. They are broadcasting it on TV. Please turn on your television, and watch my race. I will wave to you. Chow Oriana!" Carlo said briefly before he hung up the phone.

"Wait, wait Carlo. I am pregnant with your baby. Do you hear me Carlo?" Oriana responded, but it was too late! Carlo had already hung up the phone! She put the receiver down, and tears started running down her face. She watched the race on TV.

"Mommy, mommy, come sit down next to me." Oriana called on her mother.

"In the next few minutes, you will be witnessing the most important race in the world. Italy's famous racecar driver, Carlo Lombardy, has a great chance to win this race. Let's watch him getting inside his car; he is waving his hand. We wish him luck. OK, now the flag is down, and the cars are taking their first round." The sport newscaster announced.

At the end of his fifth round, Carlo exited for a pit stop. His team changed his tires, and he returned back into the race. Now, he was blocked between the drivers trying to find a opportunity to pass them. Suddenly, the announcer informed the viewers that a horrible accident had just happened. It involved Carlo Lombardy. His car went up in the air and crashed. With a crash like that, it would be a miracle for the driver to survive. Oriana covered her eyes and started to cry. She fell unconscious on the couch.

When Oriana opened her eyes, she fell into a wave of dizziness. She did not feel well. Her whole body ached. She was in the hospital with her mom beside her. She remembered what had happened to Carlo. That horrible accident! She felt sad and alone.

A nun approached her. " Glad you are up. How do you feel?" She asked looking at her chart.

"I think I 'm going to be sick." Oriana said as she sat up on her bed.

" Your condition is normal. You will be fine. My name is sister Victoria, and I'm your doctor." Sister Victoria began examining her.

Oriana felt sweat dribbled over her face, as she felt the

baby moving. "Is my baby OK?" Oriana asked her doctor with concern.

"Your baby is OK. We are preparing for your delivery. Do not push yet!" The doctor responded addressing her concern.

As Oriana's bed started to roll into the delivery room, she asked her doctor to have her mother present there. After hours of hard labor, she felt like pressure was tearing her apart. She had no longer any control over her body. Suddenly, her doctor's voice commanded "Push...... Push". She heard a tiny gurgled cry, and minutes later her mom announced happily, "It's a boy.... It's a boy!"

A moment later, a tightly wrapped bundle was thrust into her arms. There was no doubt that baby belonged to Carlo'. The baby resembled her father greatly. As a new mother, she was happy to hold him. She felt her nipples stiffen painfully, as her baby boy clasp into her breast. She turned her face away. It was a new kind of pain, as tears slide down her cheeks.

"Sweetheart, it's over at last! What are you going to name the baby?" her mother addressed her daughter.

"I love to name him Marcello, mother!" She responded with a smile.

"It's a great name." Her mother responded. "Your doctor plans to keep you at the hospital a few days, You'll be in good hands here." Her mother continued.

"Mommy, when does grandpa return home?" She asked her mother.

"He is busy filming in Spain. I don't think he will be back soon." Gina responded.

When Oriana was released from the hospital, they returned back to the mansion. A nanny was hired to care for baby Marcello during the day. Beside the nanny, three other servants, cook, and workers stayed at the mansion around the clock. Oriana revealed to her mother Gina, that Carlo Lombardy, was the father of her child, and she wished for her mother to disclose that to her grandfather upon his return.

Day by day, Marcello grew up to be a happy child. His great grandpa loved him very much, and he often hugged and kissed him. Gina loved her grandson as well. What a kind and great personality he had! Marcello's resemblance, brought back memory of his father Carlo to Oriana.

Working at the studio and coming home to Marcello was a routine for Oriana. She was not dating anyone, and wanted to make a change in her life. When Marcello reached five years old, Oriana discussed her plans with her grandpa and mother Gina. She thought moving to Los Angeles, California would be a great change for her. She could develop her plans to become a international movie star. So, they were supportive of her idea to move to Hollywood, CA.

• • •

Coming back to reality, Oriana shook away her past memories from her head. She looked down on her lap, there it was her Little son Marcello. He was still sleep comfortably, having sweat dreams. She closed her eyes, and fell asleep. A few hours later, the soft speaking pilot's voice over the microphone, reported the location of the aircraft over the northeast Arctic, while passing the Greenland. Most passengers were still asleep, but a few woke up hearing the announcement.

In the back of the airplane, there were some movements by the couple sitting next to each other. They seem to be husband and wife, but were acting very strange. Taking advantage of the passenger's sleep, the woman quickly got up, and removed her leather duffel bag on the way to the restroom.

Shortly after, she returned and stood in the back of the airplane. She was holding a machine gun, and dressed in a army uniform. Her male partner got up from the seat, and began walking toward the front of the airplane. He was holding a grenade in one hand, and a revolver in the other hand. The stewardess noticed him walk up. She tried to stop him. Using his pistol, he hit her on the head, and pusher her to the side. He reached the cockpit, and tried to open it, but it was locked.

"Open the door!" he shouted to the stewardess, motioning her with his gun.

"The door is locked from the inside, sir! The pilot will not open door until we land!" the stewardess replied, as she held her hand on her head stopping it from bleeding .

"Tell them to open the door, or I will blow up this airplane!" the man ordered, holding the grenade above his head.

"OK! OK! Let me call the captain!" she said nervously, as she picked up the phone.

"Sir, we have a situation here! There are two individuals holding the airplane hostage! One of them has threatened to blow up the aircraft, if you don't respond to their demands!" the experienced stewardess notified, as the terrorist was listening.

"Tell him that we want the release of some prisoners in Guantanamo Bay Prison in Cuba. If they aren't released in two hours, I will blow up the airplane!" the terrorist demanded, as the stewardess repeated every word.

For the security of the airplane, and safety of the passenger, there were two security men seated inside the plane. Both men dressed in casual attire, making it difficult for anyone to detect them. One of them was seated in the first class area, and the other was seated in the middle of the plane, on a isle seat. Neither one of them found any opportunity to defuse the situation right away, so they stayed put to find the best perfect opportunity.

The woman terrorist remained at the back of the airplane holding her machine gun. She was watching every passenger's move. She told all passages to remain in their seats. "Smallest movement from anyone, would trigger me to shoot!" She barked her order seriously, with her heavy British accent. As she watched her partner directly in front of her, next to the cockpit. There were no response from the cockpit.

The male terrorist was agitated! Quickly, he grabbed the stewardess and placed the revolver against her head.

"I will shoot you! Tell them again! I'm not waiting for two hours anymore! I will blow up this plane now!" The terrorist man insisted the stewardess to convey his message.

She began to cry, as she repeated his demand to the Capitan. He hit her again on the face with the revolver, as her blood spattered everywhere. She lost her balance and fell down. That was a unbearable seen for most passengers to see!

Suddenly, one of the male passengers seated on a isle seat

found his opportunity to jump on her. The security man got up to help him, when the woman terrorist shot him in the chest! He fell on one of the passengers, and began to bleed heavily. One passenger shouted, " Please help. We need a doctor!"

No one could get up to help. They were afraid to get shot. Nearby passengers helped stop the bleeding with their blankets. The terrorist woman remained calm.

Meanwhile, the captain contacted the LAX via the air traffic control tower, and reported the situation. Quickly, the captain was instructed to make a emergency landing!

Marcello woke up when he heard his mother crying. He wasn't aware of what was happening. He sat up straight on his seat looking at her. Suddenly the terrorist bent over, and grabbed Marcello's shirt. Within seconds, he was lifted out of his seat. Oriana shouted, "NO! Give me my son!"

"Sit down bitch! If you move I will kill your son!" The terrorist ordered her to sit back down.

Tim was sitting on the edge of his seat. He felt anxious, but appeared calm. He waited for an opportunity to save Marcello. The terrorist had Marcello in a headlock. He held him close and used him as human shield. The airplane reduced altitude nearing the airport, which caused the plane experience a turbulence! It was a miracle, when Marcello found his opportunity to free himself! Suddenly, he bit the male terrorist's hand really hard. The man screamed at aloud, and dropped him on the floor. Quickly, Marcello crawled toward his mother's seat, and the man attempted to shoot him. With one quick response, Tim jumped on the terrorist and they both fell on the floor. While they were struggling, the gun went off, and Marcello was shot in the foot! The grenade was dropped around a corner, under a seats.

The security man rushed to take the gun but he couldn't. Suddenly, the gun went off twice. No one knew what happened! Moments later, Tim pushed the terrorist's body off himself and stood up.

In the back of the airplane, the woman terrorist began to lose control. The male passengers found the opportunity to rush and bring her down. She fell down, and was disarmed rapidly. All passengers cheered! They were happy that the terrorists were captured and handcuffed. They felt secure when the airplane landed.

The emergency doors were opened up, and the passengers started exiting quickly. The SWAT team found their way into the plane, as Oriana screamed for help. Marcello had lost a lot of blood. The EMT began to work on the boy and other wounded men. Unfortunately, the security man shot in the chest died on the plane.

The ambulances took Marcello to the hospital. He was taken to the surgery room upon arrival. The news media, and TV reporters were standing outside the hospital waiting to hear his condition. They reported Marcello as a hero.

Tim felt a sense of attachment toward Oriana and Marcello. He accompanied Oriana to the hospital and waited. She thanked him for his courage trying to save her son's life. She cried on his shoulder, as Tim gently stroked her hair. "Everything will be OK." He told her calmly.

One of the TV reporters recognized Oriana as one of the most beautiful Italian movie stars. He was familiar with her grandfather's work, as a famous film maker in Italy and a international director. The reporter waited quietly in the hallway, as the doctor walked out of the operating room into the hallway.

"Marcello is doing well. His operation went great. He is in the recovery room right now. I intend to keep him there for observation for the next couple of days, and a few more days in the hospital." The doctor remarked.

"May I see my son?" Oriana asked with concern.

"Sure, he is sleeping right now but you can wait for him in his room. Please follow me." A nurse answered as the doctor walked away.

Oriana followed her as Tim held back, unsure if she wanted him to go there. A few steps ahead, Oriana looked back with a puzzled look. Tim understood quickly and caught up with her.

Marcello was soon brought out from the recovery room. He had an IV in his hand, and a heart monitor was attached to his body. A nurse explained that Marcello would be conscious soon.

Oriana went toward her son, held his small hand and cried. She kissed his forehead and started talking to him in Italian. Tim didn't understand a word she said, but stood silently looking at them. Hearing his mother's voice, Marcello woke up. Although weak but he managed to smile. After looking at his mother, he saw Tim standing behind her. Tim stepped closer to see him.

"You are a hero Marcello! We are proud of you. The doctor want you to rest in the hospital for awhile. When you get better, your mom and I will take you to Disneyland!" Tim told him with a smile.

"Sorry the visiting hours are over now, Marcello needs some rest. You can come back tomorrow morning," A nurse announced as she entered the room.

Oriana gave her son a big kiss on the cheek, and headed toward the door. Tim followed her into the hallway. Once outside, Tim suggested going to a restaurant near the hospital to eat lunch.

"We have been through a lot in the past few hours: the airplane ride, the terrorists, Marcello's gunshot wound, and his surgery! You must be exhausted." Tim said with concern.

"Yes I am. It's amazing how we haven't been introduced to each other formally, through it all!" Oriana said, with her Italian, English accent.

Tim nodded, and listened closely.

"My name is Oriana Rousliny. I'm a famous Italian movie star. My grandfather is the world's greatest film director and producer in Italy. I'm not married. My son's father was killed in a car accident. After his death, I was depressed and unhappy. So I decided to come to Hollywood to become a international movie star. I have always dreamed about coming to Hollywood someday. Well, here I am." Oriana explained.

"It's my pleasure to meet you. My name is Tim Forist and I'm a physician. I'm single now, but had planned on marrying my fiancé who was killed in a car accident, a few months ago. The police suspect foul play in the incident. Before we met, I spent a few years in China doing research on cancer treatment. I grew up in Los Angeles, and was returning home from a seminar in Paris when our airplane was hijacked." Tim explained, while gazing at the beautiful young woman sitting across from him.

"Glad to know you Dr. Tim Forist. Can we put aside the formalities? I like to call you by your first name." Oriana suggested with a smile.

Their conversation came to a stop, when the waitress came back to take their order. It was an Italian restaurant, and the atmosphere was very relaxed. After the waitress took the order, their conversation resumed.

"I must welcome you to the city of Los Angeles. Where are you staying?" Tim asked pleasantly.

"I have no idea, nor have any plans until Marcello is released from the hospital," Oriana replied.

"I have a suggestion," Tim said casually.

"What is your suggestion?" she asked intrigued.

"I live in Malibu. Why don't you stay at my house as a guest? You can easily visit Marcello, while he remains in the hospital." Tim asked as a great host.

"Tim I hate to impose! I owe you a lot already and prefer to find a hotel nearby until my son is released from the hospital." she rejected Tim's suggestion politely.

"Oriana, I'm positive that Marcello will be healed soon and released from the hospital. He'll be a famous boy and a hero, a little boy who saved American lives!" Tim explained, and persisted Oriana to be his house guest.

"Okay Tim you win." Oriana said with a big smile on her face.

It was sunset in Malibu when the cab arrived at Tim's house. A beautiful house with ocean view. It was a huge two-story home with four bedrooms. All bedrooms were located on the second floor, the ocean view could be seen through the stained glass windows of every room. Tim showed her a large master bedroom with a sumptuous shower. There was a sauna, and a Jacuzzi outside on the balcony. Inside the bedroom, there was a large antique wooden bed and night stands. The room was decorated beautifully with small chandelier hanging in the corner of the room, and delicate lace curtains hanging on the windows. The room had a breath taking view of the ocean, and the beach. The kitchen, living room, and dining room were on the first floor with a large spacious wooden deck off the living room door. On the patio deck, there were six chairs and a table, only fifty feet away from the ocean.

She sat on the living room couch while Tim got a bottle of wine. He sat across from her, and poured some wine in their glass.

"This is a beautiful villa. I really like it." Oriana remarked on his house with compliment.

"Thanks, this home was purchased by my parents years ago. Unfortunately, they were killed in a car accident, while I was in China. A picture of them is hanging on the hallway wall." he explained sadly.

"I'm sorry for your loss Tim. I miss my mother and grandfather too. When I left Italy, I knew that I'm entering a new world. This feels like heaven to me, living in Los Angeles is amazing." Oriana said sincerely.

"Oriana please relax and feel right at home here." Tim encouraged her.

"Thanks I'll try given the situation." She responded, as she sipped her wine.

"Life is too short and unpredictable. We have been through a lot in the past 24 hours. My best advise is that you make the best of what life bring you, and throw away what's bad from your past." Tim replied softly.

"What's your observation from us?" Oriana asked with interest.

"You are incredibly young and beautiful. A devoted mother, which is determined to do a great job raising her child. You are passionate and controlling, that's why your work comes second to you. I think men stay in the bottom of your priority list!" Tim responded summing up his observation.

"I believe some of your observation is true, but about the men in my life I have to explain that I lost my faith in them. It'll be a while before I build up my trust in them again." Oriana said, with all her conviction.

• • •

The Los Angeles Times newspaper had pictures of Oriana with her son exiting from the airplane. A cover story of how the terrorists organized their plan of hijacking the airplane, and their demands were mentioned in the article. Marcello was pictured as a little hero who saved the American passengers' lives. The

pictures of Marcello wounded on the way to the hospital was capturing a lot of attention. Some people were writing to the Newspaper, asking for rewards or medal of honor for this little hero.

The big clock in the hall way of Tim's house rang nine times.
Oriana woke up, and left the bed. She was wearing a night gown
that Tim had put in her room. She walked to the bathroom, everything inside seemed brand new. She took her night gown off to take
a shower, but changed her mind decided to take a bath instead.
She stood there naked waiting for water to fill up the bathtub.

New thoughts emerged into her mind. Thinking about how
she left Italy, with depression and sadness, but how happy she
was living in Malibu now. Leaving the safety of her mother's arms
in Italy was hard to do, but she was glad and brave to act upon
her impulses. Going over the incident on the airplane, the terrorists, and her little boy's wounded leg seemed unreal. As a unwed
single mother, she knew it's too late to look back, but she decided
to focus more on her future.

She stepped into the bathtub. The water was warm, making
her feel good all over. She leaned back and looked around the
room. The bathroom cabinets were made of polished dark wood.
It reminded her of the mansion she lived with her mom and
grandpa. She admired the workmanship. The wall decoration and
wallpaper were done in warm beige color.

Grabbing a towel from the cabinet, when she stepped out of
the bathtub. Suddenly, she saw her own naked reflection in the
mirror. She was satisfied with the shape, and curvature of her
body. She dried off, and put the night gown back on. The smell of
fresh coffee drew her to the kitchen. Tim was making breakfast,
there were omelet, toast, and fresh fruit on the kitchen table.

"Good morning Tim." Oriana said cheerfully.

"Good morning. Did you have a good night sleep?" He asked,
while pouring coffee on her cup.

"Yes, the sounds of the waves were like a mild music to my
ear. What's for breakfast?" She replied.

"Omelets! I'm almost finished." He said, as he moved toward
the kitchen cabinets.

"Please let me help you set the table." She insisted.

"OK, the plates are in that cabinet. Would you like some coffee?" Tim asked, as he pointed out the cabinet containing the plates.

"Yes please." Said Oriana.

After the breakfast, they drove to the hospital together. Surprisingly, Marcello was doing great, walking in the hall way with his physical therapist."Mommy, mommy!" Marcello shouted with joy, a he walked toward her.

She ran to him with open arms, and happily embraced him. Tim took out the newspaper to show him his picture.

"Marcello, they say you're a hero! Everybody knows you now!" Tim said.

Marcello innocently shook his head. Oriana spoke to him in Italian, just in case he didn't understand what Tim told him. She explained to him about Tim's house in Malibu near the ocean. Marcello was smiling as he listened.

"His progress in healing and recovery is going extremely well. Last night, he had a good night sleep. I think, it's OK if he continues his rehabilitation at home. I will order a physical therapist to stop by four times a week until he is completely well." His doctor disclosed.

"Thanks for everything doctor. Are you releasing him today? Tim asked casually.

"Yes, he is good to go home," the surgeon answered.

After they came out of hospital with Marcello, Tim drove to LAX airport to get their luggage back from the airline baggage center. The airport police department kept all passenger's luggage for inspection, after their airplane incident with the terrorists. They drove toward Malibu, as a unknown car started to follow them from a distance.

4

New Idea

Santa Barbara

GARY TAYLOR WAS DRIVING through the clogged freeway interchange. They seemed like the concrete lanes tangled up like spaghetti strands in a steaming pot. Especially Friday afternoon traffic congestion were extremely bad toward the direction of Santa Barbara. He hated smog and hot temperature weather.

He condemned himself to some eternal punishment, not taking the right road in his life. He was damned to travel the wrong way forever in his life!

Driving closer to home, he parked his car on the circle driveway and stepped out. Mary was waiting for him with a big welcoming kiss. He held out his arms to her, as they approached each other. Nothing looked as good as she did. He complemented her as they walked up to the front door. He didn't believe that he would develop any love for her! Now, he felt like being in love with her!

"What perfume are you wearing?" Gary asked her pleasantly.

"The one you gave me for my birthday." Mary responded with a smile.

"It really smells good. I like it." Gary said looking at her.

"Thank you honey. Are you ready to eat dinner?" She asked, as she pulled him toward the kitchen.

Raul served them wine with dinner. By the time it was ten o'clock, two bottles of wine were emptied. They were laughing and having a fun time. Gary was watching Mary's every move. She was drunk and acting very erotic. Suddenly, Mary stood up. She took Gary by the hand, and walked toward the basement. Once there, she began kissing him slowly while taking his clothes off. She made him stand there naked for awhile, not giving any indication of what trick she had up her sleeves!

A blindfold was placed on his eyes. She placed a long chain wrapped around his body. He felt the cold chain around him, allowing Mary take full charge of the whole situation. Gary stood still like a statue as he submitted to this goddess of love. The chain wasn't wrapped too tightly around him, just a little tight to hurt him and get his attention. She put the cuffs on his wrists and ankles, making him to surrender to her action. Standing back she enjoyed what was done to him.

Mary had equipped herself with a leather outfit, gloves, and costume boots. She took her leather whip, and snapped it across Gary's ass. Gary tensed up but smiled. She laid him flat on the table. With a touch of a button the table was lowered down. The chain across his chest were stretched, as she turned the wheel making the chain tightened more around his body. Now, he was shouting in pain.

"What do you like? Spanking or whipping?" Mary asked with control in her voice.

"Spanking ma lady… then I want you to make love to me." He responded readily.

Mary teased him. She could see him aroused and ready to

kneel down before her. She kissed him passionately and they made love in the basement.

The next day, they woke up close to noon. They had breakfast and coffee.

"Honey, what would you like to do today?" Mary asked, wanting to please him.

"I don't know! But I don't want a long commute to work every day!" Gary answered impatiently.

"Honey, I have an idea! How about if we turned this place into a special club for your patients? Then, you don't have to drive to Los Angeles everyday. We can remodel the house a little, and bring beautiful girls wearing leather clothes to serve members of the club! Your patients will become members by paying annual membership fee. We would also charge them per event attendance fee! What do you think?" Mary explained her plans in details.

Gary seemed interested. He nodded his head in acceptance, as he digested every details of her plan on remodeling of inside and outside of the home.

"You have a lot of interesting ideas. I like it! I will check with the City Hall for a club permit tomorrow. I'll see if I can get a loan from my bank for the remodeling. You are such a smart woman! You could be my business partner!" Tim responded thoughtfully.

A week later he obtained the business permit from Santa Barbara City Hall. Gary also secured a loan for the house remodeling. Mary found a skillful contractor who could make the changes needed to incorporate her ideas quickly.

• • •

Upon arrival to Tim's house, Oriana helped Marcello to the living room couch. Tim helped with the luggage by taking them to the second bedroom. He thought it would be good for Marcello's room to be across from his mother's room. After all, that was a temporary situation for them, and he wanted them happy.

Tim worked out of his home office for a while to make sure his guests were comfortable. Marcello was resting when he wasn't working on his leg recovery with the physical therapist. The phone rang in the living room, Oriana heard Tim pick up the phone.

"Oriana, someone is asking for you!" Tim called out to her.

"OK Tim I got it." She answered picking up the phone from another room.

"Hello?" Oriana answered.

"My name is Jamie Spring. Are you Oriana Rousliny?" The caller asked, making sure she is talking to the right person.

"Yes Jamie, what can I do for you?" Oriana asked politely.

"Miss Rousliny, I'm calling from Panther Studios, from Mr. Grant's office." The caller responded.

"Okay!" She responded curiously.

"Miss Rousliny, I'm calling to invite you to our office sometime this week. Mr. Grant would like to discuss a movie contract with you." The caller stated calmly.

"With me?" Oriana asked in surprise.

"Yes. He is considering offering you a movie contract with our studio." She responded with more explanation.

"How did you know where to find me Jamie?" Oriana asked suspiciously.

"Mr. Grant found your cover story, and picture on the Los Angeles Times newspaper." She continued on answering.

"Okay Jamie. I'm interested to visit with Mr. Grant, but I don't have a car!" She responded.

"No problem Miss Rousliny, I will take care of that for you. A limo will pick you up. Would tomorrow be a good time?" Jamie replied, trying to coordinate time.

"Tomorrow at ten o'clock, would be fine." Oriana agreed on the meeting at the studio.

At 10:00am sharp, a large white limo pulled up in front of Tim's house in Malibu. The driver who was dressed in uniform approached the door. He rang the bell and waited. A few moments later, Oriana walked out wearing a splendidly tight dress showing off her magnificent body. The driver opened the door, and made a slight bow. Oriana felt like a queen.

Instead of taking the freeways, the driver took the direction of Wilshire Boulevard on the surface streets toward Beverly Hills. Oriana got to see the Hollywood sign on top of the hill. It was for the first time in her life, seeing the Hollywood glamour and excitement close up. During the drive, sometimes the driver stole few glances of her, in his rearview mirror. She was very beautiful, like the young Raquel Welch, he thought.

"Hollywood is a beautiful city!" Oriana said, catching his glance in the mirror.

"Is this your first time in Los Angeles?" the driver asked.

"Yes, it is." she answered politely.

The driver pulled in front of a tall skyscraper. Oriana noticed a huge, bronze panther statue, stood at one corner of the building. The doorman greeted her with a smile, and opened the door. Once inside the building, a delicately beautiful girl approached her with a smile.

"Good morning, Mrs. Rousliny. Welcome to Hollywood. We spoke on the phone." Jamie said, as she stood close to Oriana.

"Thank you. You must be Jamie Spring." Oriana said, returning her smile.

As they approached a private elevator, Jamie pushed a button to the penthouse level. She explained about their company, before Oriana met with Mr. Grant.

"Thanks Jamie," Oriana replied nicely.

"The entire building belong to the Panther Company. Our company uses the top five floors, and the rest of the floors are rented to other companies." Jamie explained.

The elevator stopped, they entered the lobby. There was a receptionist, answering the phone behind the desk. The lobby was furnished with expensive leather chairs, oak desks, and beautiful paintings. There were famous pictures of actors and actresses in beautiful frames on the wall. Jamie escorted Oriana down a long corridor, which opened to a small office.

"This is my office," Jamie said pleasantly.

Oriana looked around, nodding. Then she walked toward the corner of the room, knocked on the door, and ushered her in. Jamie announced Oriana's presence, and left the room.

She was extremely impressed. Everything surprised her, and it exceeded her expectations. She felt like entering a new world, where she had to perceive as a confident woman. Immediately, she held her head high, and squared her shoulders. Looking around the dark room with dim lighting, quickly her eyes became accustomed to it. There she noticed, a short man behind the desk with four other men and two women. They were seated on the chairs around the conference room table. She stopped and stood motionless. The man appeared to be around 50 years old, short, thin, with an unattractive face.

"Mrs. Rousliny, I'm very happy to see you," Grant said, stepping away from his desk.

"Thank you Mr. Grant. I am happy to be here," she replied pleasantly.

Oriana felt like being watched by the other six pairs of eyes in the room. They were dazzled by her beauty, but no one spoke or moved. Only one women got up to check Oriana, a little closer, but did not react to her.

Looking her over, Mr. Grant treated her with respect. He felt a need to have beautiful young women with high standards, and no track records. He had a reputation for taking starlets to his home in the Hollywood Hills, promising them to be future celebrities. He had divorced his wife a few years ago, but no one knew why! Oriana remained calm and patient. She moved forward to approach him.

"Ladies and gentlemen, I think we have found the woman we've been looking for! What do you think?" Mr. Grant announced to his advisors without looking at Oriana.

"Don't you think it's best to ask me, if I'm interested in signing a contract with your company first?" Oriana snapped angrily.

He ignored her comment. Mr. Grant's colleagues knew him well. He was a rich and a powerful man who didn't really care about others' opinion.

She walked to a large window, where she could see the Hollywood sign. Standing there, she could sense Mr. Grant standing behind her. His cologne was very strong. Suddenly, she turned toward him, then stopped herself to say anything out of anger. At that moment, one of Mr. Grant's colleaguc began to speak.

"Mike, don't you think it's time to introduce our special star to the rest of us?" He said calmly, trying to break the tension in the room.

Oriana heard the words "our special star" and realized she had apparently passed the test.

"Okay, guys! This beautiful lady is Oriana Rousliny. The renowned famous Italian actress. She is the grand daughter of the most well known international film making producer/directors in the world. I saw her movies a few days ago, and her airplane hijacking story was covered in the Los Angeles Times. I plan on involving her into our future projects.

"Oriana, these are the best producers and directors in Hollywood!" Mr. Grant said with pride.

"Mr. Grant, ladies and gentleman, it is my honor to meet all of you today. I am familiar with all your names, and the movies you've produced previously. I hope to meet and get to know you in near future." Oriana responded pleasantly.

Mr. Grant gestured to one of his colleagues, to open a bottles of champagne and made a toast.

"To the most beautiful star in Hollywood!" He said raising his glass.

"May I call you 'Oriana,'" Grant asked with a smile.

"Of course!" She said cautiously.

"You may call me Mike," He responded, showing control in his demeanor.

"OK Mike. Does it mean that we are signing a contract?" Oriana asked anxiously.

"Not quite yet! There are still some conditions to be worked out!" Grant looked into her beautiful face and flashed a special smile.

"I see!" She replied.

"Is there a problem? The conditions can be easily met, it's entirely up to you!" he explained calmly.

They shook hands and he introduced his colleagues one-by-one as they left his office. He refilled both their glasses as he waited for her reaction.

"My dear Oriana, you have been a famous actress for a while in Italy now. I'm sure, you know how to make connections with high executives like me! You must accept and comply with our terms because you need me! You are a unknown actress in Hollywood, but I know how to make you famous!" Grant said, putting his moves on her.

Oriana completely understood what he meant. He wanted to sleep with her before signing a contract! Biting her lower lip, she stood up with her champagne glass in hand. She went toward the window again, overlooking the Hollywood sign. She felt helpless.

"Do you mean after you sleep with me, then we'll sign a contract?" She asked, obviously confirming his remark.

"Yes!" he shot back.

"Do you want my answer?" Oriana said in anger.

"Yes?" He replied waiting for her acceptance.

"Here is your answer!" She replied angrily, as she splashed her champagne into his face.

Oriana rushed out of his office immediately. Jamie jumped up from her desk fearfully.

"Mrs. Rousliny, is everything OK?" She asked with concern.

"Please have the limo take me home now!" Oriana demanded while shaking.

• • •

Marcello was feeling better when he woke up. It was right after his mom left to the studio with the limo. The night before, Oriana told Tim about how excited she was about her interview. She hoped to sign a contact for a movie soon and get her own place. Tim only listened not wanting to interfere into her career. They had breakfast and Tim decided to take him to Universal Studios.

Tim felt an attraction toward Oriana, and was happier with their living arrangement as house guests. His thoughts circled around her interview, after all, he didn't trust Hollywood executives, and didn't think it would be a safe haven for a young foreign inexperienced actress! He was filled with admiration for Oriana's courage, and wanted to protect her. But her beauty was exceptional as it was for; Marilyn Monroe, Sophia Loren, Raquel Welch, and other well known legendary actresses. Their beauty was breath taking and would live forever.

During their stay, Tim and Oriana mostly discussed different subjects and agreed upon some matters. It was obvious that she had become the focus of his life. Mostly Tim enjoyed hearing her verbalizing every private thoughts she had at loud in a Italian accent! She shared them with him so innocently.

Physically Tim was attracted to her as well. She had a medium height, beautiful waistline, round hips, perfect full breasts, and light complexion. Tim was devastated to hear about her past childhood story of her parent's separation, and her father's alcoholism. He remembered, Oriana telling him about her deceitful boyfriend, and all his lies in their relationship. He recalled when she cried, he took her into his strong arms and held her. That night they parted, and each went to their own bedrooms.

• • •

At the Universal Studios, people recognized Tim and Marcello from the cover story of the Los Angeles Times newspaper. The paparazzi took pictures of their every move. The youngsters flocked around them wanting to get signed autographs. They considered Marcello a hero. Realizing that Marcello was getting tired of all the attentions, they returned home. A few minutes later, he fell asleep in his bedroom. Oriana returned home quite upset and was crying. Tim tried to comfort her.

"How was your meeting?" Tim asked with curiosity.

"It was OK!" Oriana replied, not wanting to share her experience.

"I have a feeling that your meeting didn't go so well!" Tim acknowledged.

"How do you know?" She asked without looking into his eyes.

"Tell me what happened! Did he wanted to take you to bed?" He asked calmly, wanting her to explain everything in detail.

5

Actor

A FEW WEEKS AFTER THEY moved into Tim's house as a guests, Oriana had develop a deep feelings toward him. All their daily interactions together as a family, made her fall in love with him even more. The first time her heart started beating fast was on the airplane.

She found him very attractive physically. His brown eyes were bright full of tenderness, teeth were white, and his body was built strong. She loved his compassion and protectiveness. Most of all, she adored Tim's gentleness with Marcello. He treated him like his own son.

Outside the weather was changing. The wind had picked up, and blowing fast. The loud wind noise from the stormy ocean was hitting the windows hard. Oriana tossed and turned in bed constantly, not being able to sleep.

The hall clock strike one. Getting up from her bed, she left room wearing her robe. Quietly she opened the door to check on Marcello. He was deep in sleep. Feeling chilled, she looked at

Tim's room with hesitation, but returned back to her bedroom. She felt her heart surge. Walking back toward Tim's room, silently she opened the door and entered. There he was, his head on a pillow and his body covered with a blanket. Standing there for a second, she listened to the high pitched wind howling. Her mind was wrestling with her heart. She was cold and shivering. Taking three quick steps forward, she held her breath. Now, she was hovering over him trying to decide the best way to wake him up without giving him a heart attack!

She could try stroking the back of his hand but they were covered under the blanket. Not sure how to wake him up, she sat down on the floor. Her face was leveled with the mattress. She studied his face as he lay there sleeping with the covers pulled up to his chin. She thought he looked like a little boy.

Oriana was so obsessed by the design of human face. Her eyes wondered judgmentally from his chin to hairline; from his eyelids to nose; from his ears to his mouth. All were colorless in the dim light, yet each individual feature was agreeable to her. Even the nose that was too broad at its base looked solid. His features were unquestionably blunt, but their bluntness was not that of insensitivity, but of strength. His brown hair with its occasional curls was agreeable to her as well. Still with his eyes closed, Oriana decided he was better looking awake than asleep. No question about it! With an exasperated little sigh Oriana leaned forward and kissed him faintly on his mouth.

He showed no signs of waking up and was in deep sleep. She kissed him again, the kind of kiss no red-blooded man could resist even in their sleep! He opened his eyes, and moved over on his bed to make space for her.

"What are you doing here?" he asked sleepily.

She smiled clutching her robe together at the front.

"I was cold and couldn't sleep!" she said innocently.

"You're shivering!" Tim replied putting his arms around her.

"Please hold me closer, I'm so cold!" she whispered.

His arms were wrapped around her as she turned to look deeply into his eyes.

"I need you!" she said huskily.

Oriana considered herself in debt with him. She wanted to express her gratitude. The best way she knew how was to have sex with him! He didn't reply but his arms engulfed her, and drew her closer to him.

Time had ceased. The world slipped into a silent dimension in which they were the only two people there. She clung to him trembling with cold. He lowered his lips to hers as their lips touched. His tongue sought hers. Their gentle embrace grew more passionate, hotter, and deeper. His fingers felt her tight body, groped along the raised ridge of her spine. Then he moved slowly to the front of her robe. His hands slid inside to find her silky flesh, soft round breasts, and then continued slowly downward to her smooth belly. She moaned, and tightened her grip on him, as his fingers curved over her soft forest of moist hair. A tremor coursed through her body, though he had barely touched her. His finger felt her distended clitoris, and without warning slipped inside her satiny moistness. Her body arched as she released a deep-throated gasp.

At that moment, as though she was possessed, her hands began to fumble inside his silk pajamas to hold his penis. The power seemed to surge through it, and she could feel it pulsate. She could not believe how huge and hard it felt. All at once she was desperate for it!

"I want you! I need you!" Oriana whispered hoarsely.

She kissed him urgently, little moans escaping from her lips.

"Oh…. how I want you!" She said desperately in the heat of passion.

She wanted to cry out as he massaged her vagina. Touching every inch of her being, manipulating her every sensation. She thought she was going out of her mind. Their sweat mingled as one as she was his for the taking, and he was hers for the loving! Slipping out of his pajamas, he stood tall before her. It was hard for her to catch a breath, but she hungered for his love. Tim looked like a Greek God! May be more like the ideal conception of man, than real flesh and blood.

He bent over to kiss her. She Licked her lips to keep it moist and kissable. She opened her legs apart allowing him to enter immediately. He entered inside, finding her wet with desire. She started to moan as he pumped frantically faster and faster. They were as one, and the same, grasping, moaning, and monster of savage fulfillment.

Then suddenly he slowed down, afraid he might cum prematurely. He fought off the impending climax, before continuing with a steady relentless, ever-mounting rhythm. Tim was like a horseman possessed, and she wanted satisfaction! He rode her as her hips rose and fell to meet his every thrust. Twisted and twirled, greedily maneuvering her body to take advantage of his every thrust. His thrusts became fierce and furious as he moved into her deeper. She tightened her legs around his waist. There was a weak sigh in her voice as his groin touched the very lips of her vulva. The world seemed to black out completely for them, and then a cry! A burst from the depth of her being satisfied with desire. She dug her nails into his shoulders, clamped her legs together in a scissor hold. He was all the way inside, filling her completely. She moaned with each ponder, thrashing her head side to side on the pillow. She reached her climax and ultimate orgasm, as he felt the urge to release his. She was shaking with wave after shuddering wave of spasms, coursing through her body. They erupted like a volcano! The nerves shacking gloriously through their body, like volcano's after shocks! This was ecstasy!

"Wow that was great!" he gasped.

She turned sideways on her pillow to look at him.

"Will it always be like this?" she asked playfully.

"I promise, it will be much better!" he said passionately.

She smiled as she snuggled up into his warm arms. She had never felt quite as good and was totally content. Her eyes shut and her breathing became deeper. Tim looked down at her marvelous naked body and gently covered her.

Later that morning, her mind was centered on the memories of last night's love making. She took a shower and put her robe back on. Coffee and breakfast were ready by the time she entered into the kitchen. She wondered about what he thought of her, but she shook her head at her vestigial Puritanism. One thing she was sure of that she loved him.

Tim held Marcello's hand as they tip-toed quietly behind her. Oriana was standing by the kitchen sink, slicing a banana into a bowl of granola. The table was set with milk, grapefruit, toast and coffee. They hugged her from behind and she giggled.

"Oh dear you scared me!" She said as she looked around to look at them.

"Honey, we are starving!" He remarked getting ready to sit down at the table.

"OK then, breakfast is served." She replied, as she sat down too.

After breakfast, they got ready to enroll Marcello at the nearest elementary school. The principal was glad to accept a new student, specially a famous one like Marcello. His story and picture were all over the newspapers, having saved the lives of more than two hundred passengers. They agreed that Marcello should start immediately. The next day, it was planned for the school bus to pick him up. After Marcello went to school, Tim took Oriana to Beverly Hills shopping center.

As they drove around the streets, she was extremely excited. It took her breath away, how Hollywood famous people shopped there. Buying jewelry, eating in fancy dinning places, and doing spas. As they walked together, she felt wonderful holding his arm. He was a great lover, strong man, lean, and his well-muscled body excited her. His well mannered temperament made her feel comfortable and cozy.

Soon, the paparazzi started to catch up with them. Recognizing Oraina as they followed to take her pictures. The crowd gathered, and finally police had to intervene to keep them safe. Oriana was so happy and excited. She asked Tim to drive into a Italian car dealership so she can test drive a car. They greeted them and showed their latest Ferrari model. She was test driving the car when suddenly the paparazzi surrounded her car. They took pictures of her driving, which the next day appeared on the front page of the Los Angeles Times.

They returned home with two cars, Tim purchased a Mercedes and a Ferrari. She loved convertible cars! The wind blowing in her hair and body drove her wild! She was so overwhelmed and wanted to show her gratitude! A night of unforgettable sex and passion would express her feelings just great! She sat on his lap with her hands around his neck, making it hard for him to resist. He looked incredible, with tan skin, sapphire eyes, and perfect shaped mouth. She kissed him deeply.

"Do you know, how long I've been waiting for you?" She whispered.

"No tell me." He responded teasing her.

"I have never been with a man like you! In the short amount of time we've been together, it feel like I have known you for ever!" She continued, while kissing him on the neck.

"You are right! We've been together for few weeks now, but it feels like I have known you all my life!" He replied, touching her strapless shirt.

"Make love to me!" She replied, as her hands slid over his crouch.

Quickly, he picked her up and carried her to his bedroom. Their lips were locked. A woman's body has always excited him, whether slender or full, youthful or ripe. He sank his head into her lush curves, seduced by her scents. She moaned as he tore at her clothes.

She wanted to forget how Carlo's hands made her feel. Cruising over her body, Tim was the one who would make her forget! She rolled over and went on top of him. Tim was building excitement as he waited for her next move. While kissing him on the chest, her hair streamed back and forth on his stomach. They locked their hands, as she got closer to his penis with her mouth. Releasing one of her hand, she pushed in his hard penis into herself and released a sigh! She rode him fast and found release in forgetfulness. She looked down to kiss his lips again. She wanted to give herself to a man who would be there for her, and give her pleasure. She needed love and passions in her life to heal her wounds, so she can be whole again!

6

Director

Los Angeles

ELLIE MITCHELL, A FIFTY years old beautiful actress was a legendary in the Hollywood movie business. Most women envied her, and younger men desired her. She was treated like a queen, and her name was solid as gold. In a long career, spanned nearly twenty years, Ellie had known the highs and the lows of the movie business.

Separated from her husband Greg Sight, a fifty-three years old man who controlled all her activities. Ellie's friends pretended to be close to her, but she maintained her friendship with all. Her body was magnificent, but she was intelligent and clever as a fox! Still, she was all men's fantasy! A tall beautiful woman, full round breast, and light skin. Ellie believed that disappointment and triumph were like a weapon! People always respected her in Hollywood's kingdom.

Ellie was a goddess in body, but also a queen with a keen mind! Only her best friend Jessica Miller knew her best. Jessica was a widow of John Miller, who was a wealthy attorney well known in Hollywood. One day, during their conversation about a movie, Ellie told Jessica how disappointed she was with the movie script.

"Jessica, everything I have read in recent months seem to be nothing but trash!" Ellie said out of anger.

"You are a talented writer, why don't you write again!" Jessica replied, taking a sip from her grapefruit juice.

"I don't know…..!" Ellie replied, with a quick glance at her direction.

"Sweetie, everybody knows that your sexual partners are your business partners! If you haven't cared for other people's movie scripts, stop wasting your time and start writing again!" Jessica replied, urging her best friend.

Moving toward her desk, quickly she took some paper out of the lower drawer. Tossing back her hair, she got ready to write.

"Jessica my dear friend, you know me too well! I'm going to finish this new project without mentioning it to anyone. This movie script will make me a famous screen writer, and a director in Hollywood!" Ellie remarked with full confidence and intention to succeed.

Although separated from her husband, Greg Sight, they remained good friends. Greg was a well known director in Hollywood movie industry. He was the owner of Lion International Filming studio (LIF), and enjoyed living his life with glamour and glitz. He enjoyed traveling around the world, and live in a large house on the Hollywood Hills. Their second home in Santa Barbara was a villa with a great ocean view. To get away from the city, Ellie and Greg sometimes stayed at the villa to relax around the beach.

One of Ellie's passion was writing movie scripts. That's where she would let her imagination run, do her research, and gather her thoughts. As the years went by their life together went without any drama or incident. There were no kids between them, so they traveled mostly together. One afternoon at Los Angeles Airport Ellie whimpered, as they stood in the passenger's line to get her airline ticket.

"Honey I don't feel so good! Why don't you go with me!" She said not interested to travel.

"Nonsense honey! You'll be fine as soon as your valium kicks in!" Greg responded.

They were invited to a wedding. It was Ellie's sister who was getting married to her second husband. Greg encouraged Ellie to attend the wedding, but he canceled his trip with her last minute. Now, she was traveling alone to east coast! To relax on the trip, before the flight, Ellie took a valium but the pill had a opposite effect on her! She felt anxious and depressed as Greg kissed her, but she continued to cling on his arm.

"Honey don't do this to me now! I don't want to go alone!" she whispered. Ignoring her remark, Greg talked to the ticket agent at the gate.

"Can I walk her to the seat on first class?" He asked the gate agent trying to get her sympathy. She nodded and remarked, "Only for few seconds!".

As they passed through the narrow corridor, Ellie's heart began to beat harder. Her hands and knees trembled, and she leaned heavily on her husband's arm. She was afraid that her legs would give ways from underneath her, which would cause her a lot of embarrassment. Greg kept encouraging her as they got closer to her seat.

"Honey you'll be fine once the plane is in the air! It's nonstop flight to New York, and a limo would be waiting for you. Try to enjoy the flight!" Greg reassured her again.

He kissed his wife quickly, and walked out of the plane. The flight attendant was standing nearby.

"Have a good time honey. I will call you later," he said quickly.

He left before she could say any thing. He was certain, she wouldn't create a scene once inside the airplane. She was seated on the first class section, and had a aisle seat. Automatically, she fastened her seat belt and looked around. The seat next to her was empty, somehow making her feel alone and isolated! She was extremely frightened. Across the aisle from her was a man with his briefcase open. He was busy reading over some documents. She tried to take some comfort from his confidence, but couldn't. She thought, that she was going to die there!

What was she afraid of? She didn't have any traumatic past travel experience! Traveling with Greg or making a trip alone somewhere did not frightened her. There was only one bad memory that she could recall. That was when she accompanied Greg to Chicago. Suddenly, a bone-chilling panic took over her as she shivered. That flight! Touching her forehead, she realized that it was cold perspiration, and sweat building on her forehead.

"Are you all right Mrs. Sight? Can I get you something to drink?" A flight attendant leaned over to check on her.

"No thanks! I can't swallow anything right now!" She replied politely.

She heard a sound from behind but didn't want to turn around. It was a cabin door closing. Although it hardly seemed possible, but her heartbeat accelerated. She clutched the armrest, and closed her eyes. She could pretend being somewhere else, that would relax her!

The captain fired up the powerful engines, as she felt like screaming, and rush to the airplane's door. The fear paralyzed her from doing anything! She remained rigidly seated on her seat. Unable to control her thoughts, her mind returned to the flight with Greg. They had boarded their flight, and the airplane took off without any problem. When the airplane began to land at Chicago, the plane's landing gear wouldn't open! It was locked into place! Ellie could never forget the panic on the passengers face! The next few minutes followed, were terrible rush of fear making it unbearable to think anyone would live through it! It wasn't death that worried her, they were the terrible moments, as the plane plunged toward the earth, and the awful realization that a violent death was nearing, scared her out of her skin! The fact that, they could die on the plane frightened everyone! They were looking death right in the eye!

After that trip, this was the first time that she traveled alone.

Since that ghostly trip, she experienced the quiet hysteria, even though the plane had landed safely on the ground. There were emergency vehicles surrounded them, and police car's flashing lights everywhere making them feel safe. She always wondered, if other passengers on that flight suffered from the same haunting, and unreasonable fear that plagued her.

She sat quite as the slow passage of time, was only stretching her panic further away. Every little sound and movement filled her with more phobia. The Capitan's voice over the speakerphone informed passengers there would be a delay in take off! She noticed passengers had gotten out of their seats, and were standing. Confused, she signaled for the attendant.

"What's happening?" Ellie said with panic.

"There is a little delay. We have some mechanical engine problem! The Maintenance crew are checking on it now. There is nothing to worry about. It should be all cleared up in a few minutes!" The flight attended assured her.

Ellie snapped to a decision. She had been given a chance, or a leap of faith! She wasn't about to ignore it! Quickly she unfastened her seatbelt and jumped up to grab her purse. She hurried to the closed door.

"Please open the door for me! I'm not staying on this plane!" Ellie demanded from the flight attendant.

"I'm sorry lady, but we are not letting any passengers off the plane! It's only a minor…" The flight attendant responded politely.

"I said….. I want the door opened! I'm getting off this plane now!" she repeated herself. Although, she tried to keep her voice down, the words came out much louder than she expected.

The look on her face, and the quaver in her voice warned the young man not to defy her!

"One moment please!" he said, as he rushed to the nearby intercom. After a hurried consultation with the captain, he returned back.

"Just one minute please!" He said calmly.

The ramp had to be returned before the door could be opened. Ellie waited stiffly, feeling the eyes of everyone on her. She was embarrassed, and hated to draw attention to herself, but she just had to get off that plane!

At last, the door was opened. She rushed out, trying to avoid their questions as she ran toward a bathroom. Bolting through the door she barely managed to enter a stall, before her churning insides violently evacuated their contents. When it finally ended, she washed her hands as she looked in the mirror. Her face looked pale, as if she has seen a ghost!

Once outside the airport, she got a taxi cab home. It was around the rush hour traffic, and cars were driving very slow. Finally, when the cab pulled in front the driveway, she tipped the taxi driver and went inside. She lived in a beautiful home, with a spectacular view of the city lights. Everything was in perfect order as she looked around. Walking up to the second floor, that's where the master bedroom and bath was located. Half an hour later, she felt good washing away the traces of airport. The warm water had a relaxing effect on her. She wrapped herself with a soft pink cashmere robe and sat down at her make up table.

Suddenly, she heard voices from down stairs. Who could it be? She thought to herself. Silently, bare feet she walked out of her bedroom, and crossed the carpeted hallway. There was a balcony overlooking the foyer. Looking at the front door, there stood her husband Greg with his arms around a woman! Their bodies were pressed tightly against each other! He was kissing her!

Ellie stared unable to grasp what she was seeing! Sensually, the two began to grind their pelvises against one another. Their desire and passion for each other seemed to fill the air, depriving Ellie of her breath! Hypnotized, by what must surely be an illusion, Ellie couldn't take her eyes away from it all! She watched, as the woman slid her hand down to unzipped her husband's pants! She took out his penis and held it in her hand. Lowering herself to it, she placed her mouth on it!

"Don't stop!" he begged her to continue.

The sound of his voice shocked her. This wasn't a nightmare!......It was unreal! She backed away slowly going toward her bedroom. Her eyes never left the spectacle below! She knew, from the sound of her husband, that he was about to climax. She turned quickly, not wanting to witness that! They must not see her!

The coupling ended as Greg lifted her up. He kissed her and held her close.

"That was great Ann! My darling, you are terrific!" he murmured. "And soon you will be ready for round two!"

"Well thanks baby! Let's have a drink, and soon your little friend is ready again! You have to return the favor you know!" she replied.

They walked toward the wet bar together. Ellie felt betrayed. She wanted to shout at the top of her lung! What a ugly scene, she wanted to kill them both!

Softly she crept into her bedroom, and eased herself quietly into her bed. Her mind and emotions were in turmoil! This betrayal would be hacked in her mind for ever! She asked herself, "Has he done this before? Who was she? Did he love her? Does he love me? No matter what happens, he must never find out that she had seen them together!

For the second time she found herself trapped again! But this time there was no escape! If she stayed there, they would surely find her when they come to the bedroom!

She tiptoed into the bathroom quickly, and opened the drawer filled with sample medication that Greg had brought home. She could hear them talking, and laughing at loud in the kitchen. Silently, she turned the faucet handle very slightly so that warm water would trickle into a glass. She swallowed some pills with a gulp of water, and then she settled herself under the blanket. She shivered, and prayed she could go to sleep quickly.

They sat down at the kitchen table to eat some left over food Ellie had made previous night.

"Honey, why didn't you tell me your wife is a good cook?" She asked.

"Yeah, she is." Greg answered.

"Is she good in bed?" She asked playfully.

"She is fine...just not very exciting," Greg responded.

"Have you been doing it for long?" She asked curiously.

"Not long, just a few months," Greg answered.

"All these years with only one woman! How boring!" She remarked.

"Yes, only one…" Greg laughed.

"Do you love me?" She asked, putting Greg on the spot.

"Yes! Yes!" He replied playfully.

They kissed tenderly, and arm in arm they moved toward the stairs. They went up, and reached the door to the master bedroom. Greg opened the door.

"Who's that?" Ann asked, as she kept her voice to a whisper.

Greg signaled her to back out of the room. Quickly, Ann backed away. Quietly, he inched toward the bed, to confirm his fears. Yes…..It was Ellie!!! how? Why?

He turned and waved frantically to Ann to leave the house. Then, he reached under the blanket, and checked his wife's pulse. It was normal, but she was heavily drugged up! He left the room swiftly.

"What the hell is going on?" Ann hissed.

"She must have gotten off the plane after I left her at the airport!" He responded quietly.

"Do you think she saw us downstairs?" Ann asked with concern.

The thought that she might have been watching made his stomach turn. "No, I'm almost certain that she didn't! She'll probably sleep a long time with the drugs she had taken. I'll keep an eye on her till she wakes up." Greg said not concerned with the situation.

"Well, I'd better go. Call me tomorrow, when you find out what happened," Ann said hurriedly.

"Sorry about this, Ann," Greg responded.

"Yes, so am I!" Ann said with a smile.

Greg watched Ann leaving his house. What a beautiful Hollywood sex symbol! What a unforgettable time they had together!

He returned to their bedroom, and sat down beside his wife on a chair. He would know the truth once she wakes up! Did she see anything? Was their marriage over? Somewhere deep inside, a small voice whispered something, but he ignored it.

It was midnight when she opened her eyes. The room was dark and she felt weak. She remembered the event. What a nightmare! Where they still there? Her mind revolved over the scene, again and again. He looked at the clock, it was 12:30AM.

"Ellie honey, are you awake?" Greg asked checking on her. The door opened, and a shade of light crossed the bed.

"I just woke up." She replied, somehow wanted him to go away.

Greg sat next to her on the bed, waiting for more explanations.

"I got sick on the plane, and felt like vomiting. Oh…. I have to call my sister..." Ellie said in confusion.

"I just talked to her!" Greg said kindly.

Ellie felt nauseous. Greg stood up, and helped her to the bathroom. She sat on the floor but didn't threw up.

"May be if you eat a little, you might feel better." Greg asked her.

"OK I'll be down in a minute." Ellie responded feeling a little better.

After Greg left, she locked the bathroom door. She sat down on the floor in terror. Fear paralyzed her! She found enough courage to get up and take a shower. Fifteen minutes later, she joined him in the kitchen.

"Those pills gave me vertigo," Ellie said weakly.

"Why did you take them?" Greg asked in puzzle.

"I don't know! Would you help me back up to bed please?" Ellie asked her husband.

"I'll carry you honey." Greg said firmly, as he reached down to pick her up gently. She felt secure in his arms. Pressing her face against his shoulder, he carried her up the stairs.

"Honey, I'm scheduled to direct a important scene today. Are you going to be OK?" Greg said hastily.

He kissed her forehead and hurried down the stairs quickly.

Jessica Miller was worried about her friend Ellie. Looking at the wall clock, it showed 10:30AM. Usually about this time of the day, they called to talk to each other! When she didn't get the call from Ellie, she picked up her phone and dialed her phone number. The phone range several times, finally the receiver was picked up!

"Ellie…Hello…Ellie…Is that you?" Jessica asked with concern.

"Jessica?" Ellie answered weakly.

"Is something wrong? Are you OK?" Jessica asked worriedly.

"I don't feel good! I took a strong dose of medicine." Ellie replied while crying.

"Why sweetie?" Jessica asked, not sure what was happening to her.

"I don't know! I need to sleep!" Ellie replied still crying.

"Ellie! Hello! Hello!..." Jessica said, but there was no answer.

Jessica hurriedly dialed 9-1-1. She explained what happened and how worried she was about her friend. An hour later, Jessica was beside Ellie's bed, in the hospital emergency room. She took her hand into hers.

"Are you all right?" Jessica asked with concern.

Ellie opened her eyes. She tried to focus where she was at.

"It's me Jessica! What happened to you sweetie?" She asked persisting to know everything.

Ellie closed her eyes as the doctor entered the room.

"We have examined your friend and pumped her stomach. Apparently, she has taken some medication, but we are confident that she didn't commit suicide! Her condition has stabilized, and soon she will be OK." The doctor explained to Jessica.

A few hours later Ellie woke up. Next to her on the chair her friend Jessica was sitting and waiting. Ellie explained everything that happened, and saw the shock on her face. Jessica understood the drama that her friend had experienced, and she felt bad for her.

"Sweetie I have to tell you a secret! A few weeks ago, I saw Greg with a young beautiful blonde girl in a restaurant. I sat in my car, when they came out hand-in-hand. She was kissing him anxiously, when they drove away.! He didn't see me! I kept that from you because, I knew when you find out you'll be devastated. I wanted to tell you when the time was right!" Jessica explained in sympathy.

"What should I do? Get a divorce? Leave him to another woman? That's as bad as becoming a widow!" Ellie asked in confusion.

"I'm a widow. I know how terrible life can be as a single woman! Why don't you move in with me for a while?" Jessica suggested.

Ellie promised to think about it, when the doctor released her from the hospital. While Jessica drove her home in her car, she stayed quiet thinking about her situation. There were a few step which she has to take. The first step was to remain in control of her emotion, and figure out what's the best move for her situation! The second step was, not to surrender easily! The last two steps were self-reliance, and independence. She was deep in her thoughts when her cell phone range.

"Hello? Oh….. Mike Grant! How are you? Thanks for your concern. Tonight? Is it that important? OK I understand if it's necessary…… Sure I would come! OK then see you!" Ellie hung up the phone. It was one of Greg's best friends!

She had no desire to see Mike Grant, but he told her that she needs to look at some documents. Deciding to stay calm as she was getting dressed. Her mind was buzzed with plans and ideas for the new course of action. One look in the mirror gave her all the confidence she needed to go forward with her plans. It was planned for Ellie to see him at his mansion in Beverly Hills, where she had previously gone with her husband Greg Before. This was her first time going there alone. It was raining earlier in the day, but the rain had stopped once she got there. Mike had mentioned that the documents were important, but Ellie didn't know if they were useful to her.

Mike welcomed her at the front door and she felt as ease with him. She allowed him to take control of the matters he wished to discuss, so she remained quiet as he guided her to the living room. He poured some wine as she sat down on the couch. There was a file on the coffee table. Before he opened the file, he said, "There are some pictures that I have to show you! I'm sorry to say that Greg was having an affair with a woman!" Ellie stayed calm while Mike took the pictures out to show her. It appeared that Greg was out with a girl, and the picture was taken when they were kissing! Deep down inside, Ellie blamed herself for Greg's extra marital affair! She had trusted him with everything she had!

"I'm very sorry about this situation! You shouldn't have trusted him! He took advantage of your trust and betrayed you!" Mike said with all his honesty.

"Yes you are right!" She said thoughtfully.

"Would you like another drink?" Mike asked, as he got up.

"Yes, Martini please," She responded a little tipsy.

Holding her drink in her hand, she stood up and went toward the patio door. What a beautiful view! She stood there looking at the city lights, while Mike stood behind her. At that moment, she felt the urge to cry.

"I'm so sorry for how Greg treated you! He broke your heart and I know how painful that is! I want you to know that I'm here for you if you need me!" Mike remarked, as he embraced her in his arms. There were moments of silence, when Ellie looked up to face him.

"I should be going now! Thanks for your sympathy, and sharing the information Mike!" She responded quietly.

"Stay with me tonight! I want to be there for you!" Mike said, taking advantage of Ellie being vulnerable.

Suddenly, he tried to kiss her lips. She couldn't resist the temptations. His hand sled into her shirt touching her breast. Rubbing her nipples as they became hard under her shirt. Gently, he squeezing her nipple between his fingers giving it a pleasurable pain, sending a surge of desire through her spine! She moaned as his kisses became more passionate on her neck. It was like she was melting in the palm of his hand. Her mind was telling her to stop, but her inner desires told her to go on taking a revenge at any price.

As Mike tried to take her to his bedroom, she was caught in the tenderness, but quickly she pulled away.

"Mike, I have to go now!" she said, catching her breath.

He moved to take her arm, but she pulled away again.

"What kind of game are you playing?" Mike asked angrily.

"It's not a game! I'm still married to Greg! Do you know what that means?" Ellie responded, appearing very upset.

"I thought you hate your husband for what he has done to you!" Mike said, reminding her of her husband's betrayal. Without a word she ran out the front door.

• • •

Ellie packed up her personal property and left one day, while

Greg was at work. Jessica went by with a moving truck and in a few hours, they were finished moving. It took a few days for Ellie to settle down at Jessica's house and office. They seemed to be happy sharing an office together and becoming business partners.

Jessica's secretary helped Ellie set up her office. She would answer her office calls and get the mail. Every morning she brought the Los Angeles Times newspaper, and placed it on the corner of her desk. Ellie was busy reviewing her movie script when suddenly Jessica heard Ellie shout. She thought something awful had just happened to her! She rushed to Ellie's office and there she was in the middle of the room dancing cheerfully, and waving the newspaper.

"I found her! I found her!" Ellie shouted with joy, as she continued to wave the newspaper.

"You found who?" The secretary asked curiously.

"An actress for my play!" Ellie said, while showing her a picture. It was Oriana in her new car. The newspaper article's caption said, "Oriana Rousliny, the famous Italian actress bought a Ferrari!"

"Isn't she beautiful? She is the perfect actress for my movie! Go find her for me! Ask her to come see me! Make an appointment for us to meet as soon as possible. Go! Go!" She demanded, still in disbelieve.

Thoughtfully, the secretary took the newspaper and left the room. Thinking back, she remembered reading an article about Oriana and seeing her picture on the cover page of the Los Angeles Times newspaper. The story was about terrorist hijacked her plane, and her little son was the hero saving the passengers on the airplane! Doing a little research on the computer on the article, she found the story and the name of another person who was mentioned in the article. It was doctor Tim Forest living in Malibu. Looking at the yellow pages on the computer, she found his home phone number!

• • •

Oriana sat inside a huge apricot-colored tub with whirlpool jets. She was completely relaxed. A few weeks of sex and passion had cooled off considerably, and Tim was back to work. Certainly, no one could sustain the level of attention that he had given her, but fear of losing him made her sad and unhappy inside. She didn't want to drive him away, yet she couldn't stop wanting him more. It was best for her to take what she could, and enjoy making love to him under any of his rules.

A number of questions circled her head constantly. In Italy, her parents made her believe that sex before marriage was not acceptable. "The man you marry is the one you should sleep with, on your wedding night!" Her mother used to say that. In her mind, Tim was everything to her! He was the only man that she trusted and known in this country.

She couldn't forget the words Tim whispered in her ear one night, "You are a wonderful beautiful woman and I love you. You make me forget myself, with delirious joy. I don't deserve you!" Those words were too much for her.

The telephone next to her rang. She thought it was Tim, calling to say he was busy at his office, he'll be late. She picked up the phone.

"Hello? Yes, this is she. How can I help you? … With who? … Ellie Mitchell, the director? … Today? … What time? …Four in the afternoon? …Yes, that would be ok! … Let me write down your address and phone number! Thanks!" Oriana was surprised to get that phone call.

Without wasting any precious time, she got out of the Jacuzzi tub, put her robe on, and ran towards Tim's home-office. She knocked on the door, and burst right in.

"Honey, I had a call from Ellie Mitchell's secretary. She is a film director, who thinks I'm perfect for one of her movie role. I made an appointment today at 4:00PM to see her at her office. I know you are busy, but please come with me! I don't know how to get there!" She remarked and pleaded with him, while she embraced and kissed him.

"OK, do you have the address?" he asked just checking on her information.

"Yes. I have it!" She responded.

"Alright then. Let's go get ready!" He replied, when he got up.

• • •

Ellie Mitchell impatiently looked at her watch. It was nearing 4:00PM. She heard a knock on her door, and her secretary's voice.

"Mrs. Mitchell, your appointment is here! Ms. Oriana Rousliny is waiting in the lobby." Lori announced, then left the room.

Ellie sat at her desk, made herself look busy, when Oriana walked in. She was dressed, in her most elegant outfit and make up. Ellie stood up to greet her as she reached to shake hand.

"Mrs. Rousliny, glad to meet you!" she said with a smile.

"Thank you, Mrs. Mitchell. It's nice to meet you too. Thanks for your invitation to meet me." Oriana responded, while she shook her hand.

"Please sit down." Ellie invited Oriana to sit on the couch. Then she left her desk, and joined her on the couch.

A couple of knocks on the door, her secretary came in. She approached Ellie and whispered something. Ellie looked up at her and was surprised.

"Yes, if you are sure. Please tell him to join us." Ellie said at loud.

Oriana looked at them curiously, she didn't know what was going on. Her secretary stepped out but left the door open. A few second later, she ushered Tim into the room! Ellie stood up to meet him, stretching out her hand to shake hands.

"Hello, I'm Ellie Mitchell. I'm glad to meet you Mr. ..."

"Oh! Dr. Tim Forist." He said politely.

Tim was dressed extremely well that day. He shook Ellie's hand, and quietly sat next to Oriana on the couch. Ellie took a few moment, to gather her thoughts, and began talking about her movie script.

"I don't know whether, you have heard of Joan of Arc, the French girl in the history books!," Ellie began her introduction.

"Yes I have. I heard Ingrid Bergman played the role of her in a movie," Oriana remarked, interested to know more. Tim nodded his head.

Having said that, Ellie got up and went to her desk. She returned with two manuscripts.

"This is a movie script which I wrote about Joan of Arc! I have been searching to find the right persons for the role. When I saw your pictures in the newspaper, I thought you will be perfect for the Joan of Arc part!" Ellie explained honestly.

Oriana and Tim glance at each other with a smile.

"Excuse me Ellie, I'm not an actor nor do I have any experience in acting......," Tim replied nicely.

"Tim I'm sorry to interrupt. You have the look that I want for the role! The role is playing King of France, as Charles!" Ellie responded, looking directly at him.

"You mean, even without any experience you want me to act?" Tim was puzzled.

"I believe that you and Oriana are the perfect couple for my movie! I want to cast both of you in my movie!" Ellie smiled broadly and replied in excitement in her voice.

"You have surprised both of us! I have acted in many movies in Italy, including some films directed by my grandfather, Philipo-Rousliny. He is the famous international producer/director in Italy. My dream has always been to act in a movie, and portray a historical woman. This would be a wonderful opportunity, but…" Oriana replied before she was interrupted by Ellie.

"Oriana, I know what you want!" Ellie replied, then paused to think before she spoke again.

"Before you arrived here today, I did my research on your previous films. If you sign a contract with me, I offer to pay you ten million dollars for your acting. It would be five million for Tim. I want you to star in my movie, "Joan of Arc," Ellie elegantly stated.

"Really?" They shouted gladly.

"Well then, if you both agree with this arrangement, we can begin filming soon in Santa Barbara. Our film crew will stay in a local hotel, and you two…" She looked inquisitively at them.

"No. We are just friends!" Tim responded, as he guessed what Ellie was about ready to ask.

"OK that's fine with me. My secretary will take all the information and draw up our contract. It will probably take a week or so. After that we will begin with film costumes, horseback riding lessons, and other things," Ellie said happily.

"I know how to ride a horse," Oriana said proudly.

"Me too," Tim added.

"How soon should we be ready to start filming?" Oriana asked eagerly.

"I'm planning on filming to begin in mid-July," Ellie said confidently.

7

Joan of Arc

Santa Barbara

A History Deliverance

In the year 1337, the English king claimed that France should be part of England. The two countries fought, until year 1453. Around 1392, almost 55 years into the war, the Duke of Burgundy, an English man, more important and powerful than the king, decided to stop the war. In 1420, Queen Isabeau, as a representative of the king of France, signed a treaty and made peace. The Duke of Burgundy, who ruled about two-thirds of France at the time, including the north, east, south-west and Paris, told Queen Isabeau that he would have more power in the New France, and both countries would be ruled by a English king.

The French people, hated Queen Isabeau and the Duke. They didn't want France to be handed over to the enemy. The king of France, Henry V, had died and Charles VII was his replacement. He was inexperience, and his treasury was empty. He desperately, needed to find money to pay his army to fight against the English. Then, a miracle occurred. From a humble village called Domrémy, a peasant girl was born around year 1412. . Her parents were farmers. She was named Jeanne. She was still in her teen years, when she set out on a quest that would change the course of history. Later, she became known at Joan of Arc.

• • •

After Tim Forist's passed his movie screen testing as King Charles' character, Ellie's mood was upbeat. The film production was shaping up perfectly well. She wasn't sure, whether she would use all the written material in her script, but felt great how her crew relationship was developing. She strongly believed, that the story of Joan of Arc would be in a high category of movies winning the Oscars.

It was early in the morning, on a hot month of July when the filming began. For make up and costume fitting, Oriana reported in at 6:30am. She was seated in front of a mirror in her mobile home trailer. Her first scene required her hairdresser to put the wig on Oriana's head. One look at herself in the mirror, she was confident about her appearance.

"I have never been in a mobile home trailer before!" she remarked to the hairdresser.

"It's your for the duration of filming. You'll get used to it." Her hairdresser assured her.

There was a knock on the door, a assistant director was checking on their timing.

"She is ready!" the hairdresser responded.

Oriana opened the door, and found Ellie standing nearby.

"Am I late?" she asked with a smile.

"No, no, you are on time. You look just like 'Joan of Arc!" Ellie responded with a puzzle on her face.

To get closer to the location of film shooting, the vehicle was driven down with all casts and crew. The road was narrow, and the overgrown bushes were framing the roadsides. There were shrubs near the small river, close to the farmers' huts. It was the exact replica of the location, where Joan of Arc previously lived. Oriana was very impressed by what she saw, and imagined Joan's family and how they lived. The caravan stopped in one corner.

• • •

"The future savior of France, Joan of Arc, was much like all the other girls in the village of Domremy. She was an ordinary peasant child, sunburned and strong. She worked hard sometimes, to help her father on the gardens and fields. Other times, she stayed home with her mother and did house work." Oriana imagined how Joan of Arc's life style would be like.

Joan's father, Jacques D'Arc, was a leader in the village. The family lived in a stone house, close to church. Their home had a dirt floor, and the rooms were damp and musty. There was no bathroom, or shower for them to clean. Her mother and father were strict with their five children. None of them could read or write. The only education she ever got was from her mother, Isabelle. Their parents took them to the church, to be a good Catholics. Joan was extremely bright, learning her lesson well at church. Her friends teased her about it.

The people of the village were intensely loyal to king Charles. The village was a narrow strip closed to Burgundian territory, on one side, and Lorrain territory, on the other side. The village was mainly cut off from France. They had protection from the English, but Burgundian soldiers burned people's houses, and stole their livestock. The war was very real to Joan, and all people knew who the enemy was!

When Joan was about thirteen years old, one day, she started working in the garden alone. It was around noon time, when the church bells rang. Suddenly, she heard a voice from behind her. Quickly, she turned to see who it was. Then, she saw a bright light coming from the saints. She froze, but never told anyone about the voices and spirits she saw. Again, they came to her for the second time, another day. By the third visit, she saw through the light. It was Saint Michel! Later on, other

Saints came to her as well, but she knew them because of their statues in the church! She continued going to the church, and loved seeing the visions. Sometimes, she cried when they disappeared, leaving her with a lot of questions on her mind. It's important to remember, that she lived in a time, when even educated people believed in fairies, curses, prophesies, witches, and magic. They were deeply religious, and accepted the unexplainable, much more readily than we would today.

As Joan grew older, her visions began conveying distressing matters. They spoke about misery in the kingdom of France, and told her that God had a mission for her. She had to leave her village, and travel through the enemy's territory. She had to reach the King Charles's army, and convince them to follow her, on the dangerous journey, north to the cathedral at Riems. That's where he would be crowned as the King. She didn't understand how she could fulfill that request, for she was just a poor girl, who didn't know how to ride a horse, or lead an army in war!

Joan's father wanted to arrange a marriage, but she said, she would "never get married". Shortly after her seventeenth birthday, there was a prophesy. Widespread at the time, that France would be lost by a woman, and saved by a virgin. Everybody knew who the woman was, the Queen Isabeaue. She urged the poor people, and drove the King mad to sign away his country. Could it be, this poor country girl destined to save France?

The history has it, that there was one event that may have finally had tipped the scales! The French army were losing another battle to the English army, somewhere near Orleans. A few days later, messengers arrived with news of the disastrous battle. It had been just as she had foretold. The governor gave her his blessing.

Joan began to consider some practical questions. How would she dress?. A woman riding across a dangerous country, would be a target for attack! Besides, if she was to ride with an army, then she must dress appropriately, in men's clothes. The people soon pitched in, giving her a tunic, hose, boots, and spurs. Also, they gave her a horse, and provided a sword. To complete the picture, Joan cut her long hair short.

On a cold evening in February, Joan's great journey began. She rode out of the city, with an escort of six men, including the two young noblemen who had become her supporters. One of them, even paid for the trip. It was three hundred fifty miles to Chinon. The first part of it, was through English army's territory. To avoid enemy soldiers, they traveled at night, skirting towns and villages. The danger didn't end, even when they reached France. There were robbers to fear, and pass over icy rain, with swollen rivers.

Joan had never ridden any horse, except a carthorse around her village. She proved to be a natural horse woman. For the next two years, she was rarely out of the saddle. Nearing Chinon, Joan stopped at the little town, and sent a letter to King Charles. She wrote in the letter, that she would soon arrive there, and asked for a meeting. A shrine for prisoners of war was set up, and the walls were covered with swords, chains, and armors. They were left there, by soldiers who were grateful for their release.

Finally, after eleven days on the road, the small band continued on the short distance to Chinon. They arrived there about noon time. People passing by, stopped to look at them. The whole town had talked about a story spread through France, about a miraculous maid. It was evening, when Joan was escorted up the steep cobblestone streets of Chinon.

There is a old story about, when she passed by, one of the guards made a rude remark. Joan snapped back, that he was mocking God with his insults. She said, "You are so near your death." It's very easy to imagine, how such a small tale could make the rounds of Chinon, before morning!

Entering the grand chamber, Joan was dazzled by a spectacle of color and light. Over three hundred nobles filled the hall. Their brilliant silks, and velvet gowns, glowing in the torchlight. All of them watched her with fascination, for she had boasted, that she would know King Charles instantly. Although, she had never seen him, but she was being tested! Somewhere in that splendid crowd, Charles hid. His clothes did not set him apart from others, nor did he look kingly with his large nose, and sleepy eyes. Joan headed straight for King Charles, as if he were an old familiar friend.

"God give you life, gentle king," she said.

"I am not the king Joan! There is the king." He pointed to another man, but she was not fooled.

"By God, gentle prince. It's you and none other, true heir of France, and the king's son!" She remarked, standing before the king.

Then, withdrawing from others, Joan gave Charles a sign, to prove she came from God! No one really knows what the sign was, but witnesses said ,as she spoke, his face grew radiant, and he was changed!"

• • •

After a week of filming, and working from dusk to dawn, Ellie's crew were making lots of progress on shooting the village scenes. The crew returned to the production's headquarter at Santa Barbara's hotel.

"I'm so excited about Oriana's work today. She's a great actress!" Ellie told her secretary.

"Mrs. Mitchell, I feel so honored to work for you. I believe your film could win the Oscar!" she said honestly.

"Yes, I think so too!" she replied, deep in her thoughts.

Ellie's cell phone range suddenly. She picked up to answer the call.

"Hello?...... Mary?" She responded in shock.

"It's my niece! My sister's daughter Mary!" She announced to her secretary. She put her hand over it while answering the phone.

"How are you honey? How is your mom? I'm really sorry, I couldn't make it to her wedding. Is she happy with her new husband?" Ellie asked making conversation with her niece.

"Oh yes...... he is younger than your mom! What are you up to lately?" Ellie asked, out of genuine interest.

"What? ...You are inviting me to......? Are you getting married? Not yet, huh? Dr. Gary Taylor? No, I've never heard of him! Who is he? … A professor of sexual psychology?" she asked teasing her niece.

"So where are you inviting me to? The grand opening of a club? What kind of club?" Ellie continued asking curiously.

"Mary, are you kidding me? I'm sorry honey, but I'm really busy shooting a movie! Where is the club? Santa Barbara? That's where we're shooting at! OK, let's see if I could come by! Give me your phone number! OK Chow for now honey!" Ellie ended the conversation wearily.

Back at Tim's house, everything was peaceful and quiet. The bed felt safe, as her body turned over to face the warmth that emanated from Tim. Feeling her body next to him, as he spooned her from back. Closing her eyes, she wished this was all there was to life! Warmth, comfort, and touch! Sharing a bed together with someone that you love was the nicest feeling. She had never known how that feels, and how much pleasure one can have sleeping next to their partner.

It had been three months since they met. It was she, who altered the pace of their relationship, and whipped the speed of passion. Their bed was full of dangerous delights, which echoed with whispers, demands, and broken moans.

Outside, the sun was swallowed up. She turned over against his back. He moved slightly as she put her arms around his waist, and snuggled up closer. She didn't forgot the feeling of the first time they made love. She was overwhelmed with the thoughts of it. It was him, who helped her discover her body! She nuzzled her cheek against his back. His skin had cooled, but her warm body balanced his body temperature.

Suddenly, the bedroom door opened up, and Marcello came in. He was rubbing his eyes.

"Mommy, mommy!" He said, as he entered the bedroom.

Quickly, Oriana moved over on bed opening space for Marcello to climb in. She gave him a warm kiss on his cheek as she pulled up the bed cover.

"Marcello, it's early in the morning! Why are you awake so soon?" Oriana asked with concern.

"I don't know," Marcello responded.

She began to stroke his hair gently, and soon after he fell asleep again. Tim got up from the other side of the bed. One hour later, she got up and went down to the living room. He was standing by the window and looking at the ocean. Lost in his own thoughts, he was drinking a cup of coffee. He didn't hear Oriana walk in. She took a large step toward him and wrapped her arms around his waist.

"A penny for your thoughts?" Oriana said playfully, waiting for his response.

"When I think about my childhood years and relationship with my parents, I remember how much they loved me. When Marcello came into our bedroom this morning, it brought back memories of how I was in that age! I guess, I have to accept the fact that Marcello needs you as much as I do!" Tim shared his inner thoughts with her.

His words made her realize more clearly. They broke down all her walls, and put her thoughts in perspective. Now, she could see into his heart! What a special man he was! She remained quiet.

"My dear Oriana, my wish is to keep our relationship last forever! This morning I realized that it's impossible for me to live without you! You bring so much happiness to my life, and for that I'm grateful to you! I love you!" Tim had tears into his eyes, as he expressed how he felt inside.

"Honey, I'm so happy to have you in our lives. No man has ever treated me the way you do! I love you too!" Oriana replied honestly looking into his eyes. "Let's spend some time together today. Just the two of us!" She continued on with so much love and affection for him.

After breakfast Marcello went to school. There were no movie shooting planned for that day. It was a beautiful day to drive up the Pacific Coast Highway. The whole day, she watched her boyfriend with admiration.

"What do you think of my acting honey?" Oriana asked, wanting his honest opinion.

"I think, you are a highly talented actress!" he answered seriously.

"Really?" Oriana asked, looking at his face.

"Really! You are as beautiful as Marilyn Monroe, and as talented as Ingrid Bergman, should I go on.......!" He responded, taking his eyes off the road for a few second.

"Also your velvet eyes are the first things that attracted me to you!" He continued on as she remained quiet.

"I'm so glad that we work together, filming this movie. Being near you makes me happy, and brings our relationship closer together. We have a scene together tomorrow! My best advice to you is, to have self-confidence and trust in yourself!" Oriana shared her thoughts.

"Thanks for the great advise honey." Tim replied with a smile.

• • •

King Charles was still cautious. Before he put the French troops in Joan's hands, he wanted to be sure her voice came from God, not from the devil. He sent her to a church council to be examined. Week after week, the questioning dragged on, and Joan grew restless. One day, she said, "I have not come to prove the sign! Take me to Orleans, I show you the sign from God.

In the end, the Church council found nothing. They advised King Charles to trust her. To the amazement of the people, the King ordered for Joan be lodged at a tower in the castle. She was treated with respect. She was given a suit of armor, and a better horse. To obtain a better sword, she sent her servant to a chapel, where she could pray for a special one. Then, she told him "There is a special sword buried behind the altar. No one has ever heard of such a sword!" The sword was found, just as she had predicted to everyone's surprise. Also, she had a banner to show the soldiers, where she was at all times. She thought, it would protect her from getting killed.

King Charles raised an army, with the financial help of his mother-in-law. It was dispatched to release in Orleans. The people of Orleans rejoiced. They heard, "an army was coming to their rescue, led by the saintly maid of God!" The truth was, that Joan wasn't the commander of that army, she was the captain. Joan was the true heart, and soul of that army, and she looked after its spiritual well-being. She made all the soldiers go to confession, and wouldn't allow them to swear. Joan told the men, to be merciful conquerors, never burning villages, or steal from the people. They must do nothing to displease the King in heaven. She told them "The army would fight the battle, but God would grant the victory".

The Duke of Orleans, would have led the defense of his city, but he was a prisoner in England. Instead, his half-brother was in command. The army, with cart loads of food, and herd successfully entered into the city. This plan was possible, because the English forces had few men around Orleans. Completely leaving the East gate unchallenged , much of the time, it was late in the evening, when the citizens filled the streets with joy. They cheered as Joan's army passed by. A spirit of hope, was in the air! While waiting for reinforcement, Joan sent several letters to the English army, urging them to go back to their own country. Joan dictated the words, and someone wrote the letter. Because she never learned how to read or write, she signed the letter as "Jehanne" by mistake. The English army thought her letters were total rubbish, and responded back by saying, "It's better if you go back home, and mind the cows!"

Still determined to prevent bloodshed, Joan decided on a more personal appeal. She rode through the south gate of the city one day, and out onto the bridge over Loire River. Guarding the far side of the bridge, there was a stone fort, in the hands of the English. To keep the English army from crossing, the French had destroyed a section of the bridge. Joan shouted across, to the English army, persuading them to abandon the fort immediately. They hooted back, "Cow girl!"

The French high commander, the Dunois, didn't take her seriously either. The next day, Joan and the army rode out to attak the English army, with their spirit high. Joan fought, side by side, with the French army, and it's captain. In fact, she was the first person, who set a ladder against the wall. They climbed beneath a rain of arrows, only to be repelled at the top, by English swords and battle axes. At about mid-day, Joan was hit by an arrow in the shoulder. Her men carried her to safety. She pulled the arrow out herself, and rested only a short time, before returning to action.

Night time came, and after thirteen hours of fierce fighting, the men were exhausted. Joan pressured the army's captain Dunois, to keep fighting because the victory was theirs! He agreed. Joan picked up her sword and carried it to the edge of the moat. The army could see her determination to win the war, so they joined her. The English defenses broke down, and the French army poured over the walls unhindered. The English were unaware that the French had stationed a boat under the bridge. It was set on fire by the French army, as the English army began to cross the bridge. The bridge collapsed in flames.

It was May 7, 1429, when that led to a stunning victory for the French army. From that moment, the people of Orleans celebrate that glorious day every year.

The next morning, Joan rode to the Dauphin's castle. King Charles was so pleased to see her. He kissed her with joy. After two weeks, the army set off to clear the way, for the march to Reims. The English forces had been rebuffed by the French army. More than four thousand English men were killed or captured by the French army. Lord Talbot, the English commander was taken as a prisoner. However, the French army, lost only three men.

• • •

An article about the Joan of Arc movie was written in the local Santa Barbara Newspaper. The story was written about the shooting of the movie in that location, and how it has helped boost the local economy. It was reported that, Oriana Rousliny, a brilliant 25-year-old Italian actress was playing the Joan of Arc role. Also, Tim Forist, a newcomer actor was playing the King Charles. The newspaper story talked about Ellie Mitchell, who as a famous Hollywood actress, was directing her first film there, and had discovered them both!

The reporter indicated that Ellie Mitchell, married to her famous husband Greg Mitchell, is accepting the big responsibility of directing the movie. Her movie fans, expect a lot from her as the director of this movie. The reporter mentioned in the article, "People have high regards for her, in spite of separation from her husband Greg."

The production of the movie had cost Ellie Mitchell a lot of money. She had borrowed unheard amount of money, and asked her investors to stay supportive of the film. She was smart not to have a major female movie star play the role. That way she saved her money, and carried the glorious flag all the way to the bank! She was aware that, her film could be among the best movies nominated for the Oscars that year! Deep inside, she wished that Oriana could be the best actress nominated for the Oscars as well!

The second week of filming was finished. Due to the ungodly work hours, Oriana had become quite good at getting whatever rest she could, during each movie takes. She often napped in the limo, driving to and from work.

One afternoon, Ellie had a special meeting with Oriana, Tim, and entire crew. Upon arrival there, they noticed some posters on the wall. Ellie seemed to be excited, and was impatient to discuss things.

"I have to thank all of you! This movie could not have happened without all of you! This was my dream, that some day I could direct a movie this caliber. I admire all your efforts, passion, and hard work to make this film successful. My prediction is that, Joan of Arc will be the biggest picture of the year! We have a very difficult week ahead of us, and I want everyone to continue their hard work. Please go over the script, re-read and rehearse your lines. " Ellie remarked, showing her gratitude.

"Is there any questions?" Ellie asked all attending the meeting.

"Do we have the budget for marketing and advertising?" One of the crew members asked.

"Great question! I will do what it takes to plan our budget carefully on marketing of our film. Meanwhile, my plans are to get as much as press coverage that we can! The more public hear about the film, the more they get interested to go see it, once finished. Let's make a video of our production behind the scenes as we're filming! Also, pencil into your calendar, next Saturday night! We are having a big party at the hotel, with live band for publicity. The local press and reporters are invited!" Ellie continued with excitement.

There weren't much spare time in Ellie Mitchell's life. She

attended every shooting in every scene. From the moment she got up in the morning, until late at night she was busy with directing, producing and editing of each takes with the crew. They began filming in a new location. Oriana was working with Tim on his lines every day. She made him practice every scene alone, and they practiced together again later in the day. The crew worked with him as well, and practiced before every shooting.

At the end of each day, Ellie received the film negatives taken from the scenes and reviewed them for editing. She wanted to make sure the film progressed well. Tim Forist's acting was improving daily, and Ellie was happy about that. He had finally gotten himself in front of the camera, and the result was brilliant. Although, Tim didn't have experience in the movie industry, but slowly he was getting comfortable in front of the camera. The negative of his shots, were outstanding! Somehow, his personality was shining through his work! His eyes were full of honesty, giving the film a twist of reality.

The week went by quickly. At the hotel, the staff were preparing for the special party planned for the film production. They worked hard to make a special, and unforgettable night. A giant tent was placed outside. There were fifty tables set, covered with white tablecloths, and red roses were centered on each table. There were candle lights everywhere. The walls of the tent, were covered with different posters of the Joan of Arc movie, and many sparkling lights twinkled on the ceiling of the tent.

There were so many people attending the party, making it difficult for Ellie to make her rounds. Oriana and Tim accompanied her as well, as she introduced them to most of her movie star friends, directors, producers, and her best friend Jessica Miller, and Mike Roesel. Ellie was trying to make sure everyone had a good time. She checked on reporters and news media to make sure they have enough material to do their story. Publicity was the key to her film's success! The rest of the night, everyone enjoyed their time dancing, drinking and relaxing.

Dinner tables were set ready for guest's seating. At the main table, Ellie sat with Oriana and Tim, her best friend Jessica Miller, and a few other important guests. She sipped her wine as they talked. The reporters and TV station broadcasters were covering the event closely.

On one corner, Mike Grant gazed around waiting for an opportunity to talk to Ellie. He was Ellie's husband best friend, who had strong feelings for her. Ellie had four glasses of wine as she signaled the server to give her one more. She felt good and carefree. Standing on her feet all day, she took her shoes off and held them in her hand. As she walked toward her room at the hotel, she passed by Mike Grant.

"You're the world's sexiest woman here! How do you feel?" Mike remarked flirtingly.

"Oh, Hi Mike! I'm doing fine!" She said stopped for a moment.

"Great! I have heard that you've got some budget problems! May be I can help!" He asked, attempting to get her attention.

"Not yet! But I think I'm getting there! It's going to be an expensive movie, you know! Excuse me, I was on my way to the restroom! But I'll be back!" She said without waiting for a response.

She was wearing a beautiful backless dress. It was a see through black long dress, which revealed her round full breasts in the front. Unable to walk straight, she left the tent despite all the faces looking at her. She reached her room and entered. Walking directly to the bathroom, she forgot to close the door. Mike had followed her, and noticed that her door was open! Quietly, he entered the room, and closed the door. Standing near the bathroom door, he heard water running in the bathroom sink. Suddenly, Ellie walked out of the bathroom, and screamed frantically when she saw him.

"What are you doing here?" she asked furiously.

"You know why I'm here! I want you!" Mike replied clutching her hand.

Ellie was an accomplished actress, but this was a awkward situation. She knew men found her very attractive, but this was very strange!

"Please Mike!" Ellie responded as she pulled away from him.

"Tell me what you want! Do you want my apology!" he said desperately.

"For what?" Ellie said with surprise, keeping her eyes on him.

"It's something I have to say! I know you have been separated from your husband Greg, and don't have anyone else. I could be…" Mike said, trying to make sense of his words, but was interrupted by her.

"Mike, for heaven's sake, this is ridiculous and nonsense!" She replied, moving toward the door to open it.

"I know how unhappy you are. Let me make you happy…" Mike tried to reason with her.

"OK Mike that's enough! I don't need any man to make me happy! Get out now!" Ellie ordered as she tried to control the situation.

Mike left her room and Ellie returned back to the party. She held her glass of wine in her hand as tears were running down her eyes. Quickly, she brushed away her tears, deep down she knew the only man who could make her happy was her husband Greg! Now that the destiny has changed the course of their life, she must accept and move on.

8

The Torture Club

Hollywood millionaire Mike Grant was heart-broken at his inability to win Ellie Mitchell over at the party. She was his best friend's wife, and he had the biggest crush on her. Despite their two recent meetings, they just weren't connecting. He planed to make a trip to Santa Barbara seeing his doctor, Gary Taylor! He was the famous owner of the Torture Club! Something there had attracted his interest. Secretly for a long time, he had been one of Dr. Taylor's patient!

The club was built with a modest white stucco exterior. The interior was elegantly decorated with sharp colorful paint and nice carpeting. A DJ was playing loud music, with flashing lights all around him. The staff were dressed in while gloves, no shirt, tight leather pants for men and tight leather skirt for women. They served the clients with their beautiful smile, and hard tanned bodies.

As Mike entered the club, he was given a choice between a black or a white mask. To make club members happy and to hide their social status, the club kept the identities secret.

The guests were welcomed individually by Dr. Gary Taylor and greeted by Mary as they walked in. Mary Fawcet, his girl-friend, as the second host made sure that the members were familiar with the rules of the club. She was wearing a sexy outfit showing her cleavage. Mike kissed her hand, and told her how beautiful she looked. He made a pass at her, but she didn't take it seriously.

"It's so lovely that you could join us! We've been expecting you! Let me introduce you to my friend Lucy! She will take care of you!" Mary welcomed Mike personally as he was escorted away.

Lucy guided Mike to a privet room. There, she ordered him to take all his clothes off. He didn't argue and did what he was told to do! She wrapped a long chain around his body, but she was careful not to hurt his penis. The chain wasn't too tight to make him uncomfortable. Lucy knew about Mike's history with Dr. Taylor because she read his file earlier in the day. Mike liked to be degraded!

"Are you stupid?" she asked with authority.

"Yes ma lady!" he replied, not making any eye contact with her.

"I'm not your lady you fool! I am your Mistress Lucy! Are you a coward!" She asked, walking around him.

"Yes, Mistress Lucy." He answered quietly.

"Kneel over there slave!" she demanded, pointing her finger to the corner of the room.

He followed her instruction as two other women came into the room. They were dressed like Lucy. Topless with tight leather short skirt on. They carried a leather whip as well. One of them approached Mike, and snapped her whip across his ass. He didn't make a sound but was frozen in place. The other girl, made him bend over! Then she climbed on his back and rode him like a horse! Mike continued eyeing Lucy in the center of the room. She pulled his chain making him stand up on his feet. Then, he was taken to a huge wooden shape cross. There were leather strap handcuffs attached to them.

"Have you been a bad boy slave?" Lucy asked, acting as his master.

"No, Mistress." Mike answered desperately.

"You are a liar! Are you comfortable?" Lucy asked circling him.

"Yes, thank you Mistress!" Mike answered quickly.

"Do you want to be spanked or whipped?" Lucy asked for his punishment's preference.

"Don't look at me so innocently you fool!" She snapped, when he looked at her anxiously.

"Yes Mistress. I like to be spanked!" He answered hesitantly.

"I'll spank you slave! Are you ready?" She replied, as she positioned herself toward his back.

"Yes Mistress!" He answered, waiting to be spanked.

"Crawl to me, you pathetic excuse for a man!" She ordered him.

He crawled and waited. She gestured to the other girls to leave the room. She spanked his ass a few times then stopped. His skin had turned red, but there were no bleeding.

"Please take this chain off Mistress!" He pleaded with her.

"Not until I am ready!" Lucy snapped her leather whip, letting him know she was in charge.

"Please don't hurt me anymore!" He begged her to stop, when she got ready to spank him again.

"Do you like my boobs? She asked, ignoring his previous remark.

"Yes, Mistress, they are beautiful!" He answered honestly.

"Okay Then. Let's proceed with sex!" She remarked knowing he was ready for the next step, according to the club's rules.

• • •

The Royal army moved north, as the town opened their gates without a fight. The enemy soldiers from England, feared Joan of Arc. Two weeks later, when the army arrived in Reims, the townspeople offered full obedience to their sovereign.

The French army, and Joan rode together to the Dauphin's castle, on May 7th, 1429. King Charles was so pleased . The Loir campaign was successful. King Charles, later with his royal army, moved north. They knew Joan's reputation had cleared the way for them to victory. The town's gates opened up without any fight. Throughout the England's territory, the soldiers began to desert in fear of the Maid.

King Charles reached Reims, at 9 o'clock of May 17th, 1429. The grand procession, made its way on oath, to uphold the Catholic faith, defend the church, and rule his kingdom with justice and mercy. Then, the king was knighted by the Duke of Alencon. King Charles received the scepter, a symbol of authority, which he held in his right. Finally, the Archbishop laid the crown of France, on Charles's head. Joan knelt proudly, and wept with joy, in her hand held standard. Later, when they asked why she had been given such a place of prominence in the ceremony, she answered, "She had borne the burden, and she deserved the honor."

The king rewarded her by raising her family to the nobility. He also granted, the only favor she asked for! Her little village, be exempt from taxes forever! Her mother, father, and two brothers, were witnessed the ceremony.

On July 17, 1429, at nine o'clock in the morning, the coronation in the cathedral began with prayers and music. King Charles swore to defend the Church, and rules of his kingdom, with justice and mercy for all.

Now, a great moment of decision arrived. Joan's miraculous victories were the talk of France. King Charles had been properly crowned at Reims. Throughout the North, cities that had long lain under Anglo-Burgundian control, were ready to submit to him. King's army on the other hand, was eager to fight; to take back Paris. They wanted to drive the English out of France altogether. However, King Charles had hopes of ending the war, by winning the Duke of Burgundy, and run his English alliance away.

Without telling Joan, he agreed to a truce for fifteen days. During which, Burgundy promised to give up Paris. The Duke did not reveal, that 3,500 knights and archers, had already left England, to reinforce in Paris. After three weeks, king Charles decided to attack, although he knew Paris was now well fortified, and protected by a moat.

To prevent bloodshed, Joan called upon the defenders to

yield quickly. An English archer let fly an arrow, and it pierced her thigh. She was carried from the field. The French army, withdrew that night.

The following morning, before the battle could resume, a message arrived from King Chares, ordering them to abandon the fight, and return back. This was a terrible blow. King Charles had decided to retreat, so the French army left, and headed south of Paris.

King Charles spent six months time, hoping that the Duke of Burgundy from England, would play fair for peace. So, he did nothing, while more English soldiers crossed the channel to France, and took back all of what he had gained previously.

Joan didn't wait for King Charles to realize his mistakes. She joined a small band of mercenary soldiers, and headed north to fight the English army.

At the beginning of her mission, the holy spirits told Joan that she would last only a year! Now, the voices were telling her, that her time was up, and soon she would be captured! Having knowledge of her prophecy, she learned that as part of the truce, King Charles had given the city of Compiegne, back to the Duke of Burgundy from England. The French people had refused the treaty, saying they would rather lose their lives, and their wives and children, than to expose them to the mercy of the Duke!

Deeply moved by that story, Joan rushed to their defense with about four hundred men. She slipped through the enemy lines by night, and entered the city. The next afternoon, she rode out the north gate, with a small force of soldiers, to attack a Burgundian encampment, on the far side of the drawbridge. The enemy caught by surprise, retreated hastily. As the French army galloped in pursuit, they suddenly found themselves ambushed, and in danger of being cut off from the town. Joan tried valiantly to convince her men to fight, but they went racing back, allowing enemy soldiers to surround her! One of them grabbed her cloak, and pulled her off from her horse. Now, she was a prisoner!

• • •

Almost a month of filming had gone by. Ellie slouched comfortably on the sofa in her room, inside the hotel. She was exhausted from the long day's work, and wanted to relax. All her film crew were tired too, they worked long hours. It was the fourth of July holidays, and she thought it would be a good opportunity to look at the budget from various departments.

Oriana had thrown herself into the film's character. It seemed so amazing, that the destiny had lead her to play the role of Joan of Arc. The role was so perfectly tailored for her. Oriana was known to be the Naples Goddess. A young beautiful woman, who was strong and passionate about life. All the characters that Oriana and Joan of Arc had in common. It was pure luck, and the grace of God, which Ellie discovered Oriana to play the character.

One morning, when Tim woke up instead of getting out of bed, he continued resting beside her. The scent of her skin, heated with passion, drifted through his senses and merged with the fragile fragrance of the camellias. The sun light shadowed by the blinds, seemed neither day or night, but of some timeless space hidden between. Captured in his arms, her body moved gently with each quiet breath she took. Lifting his head up, he could see the glow of passion still flushing in her face. He had only to kiss her to taste those warm and sweet remnants of mutual pleasure.

Slowly she opened up her eyes and let her fingers comb through his hair. Giving him a kiss on the lips, she struggled to get up.

"You look sensational darling! For brunch, I suggest we take Marcello out some place special!" Tim remarked considerately.

A beautiful sunny day in Santa Barbara. As Tim pulled up in front of a Persian restaurant in down town area. Once inside, she couldn't help but wonder about how exotic the interior of the restaurant was! There were Iranian luxury items, small rugs, a few beautiful paintings decorated the walls. One of the paintings attracted her attention, as she got closer to it. It was a painting of a coffee house with magnificent gold engraving on the frame. It went back to 1400 years ago. She couldn't believe her eyes, as she gazed at those luxurious antique pictures.

"Dear guests, welcome to our humbled Persian restaurant.

Would you please follow me?" A waitress in Iranian garments led the way.

She looked over the table, where normally eight people would be seating, but it was set for three. She realized, it was a table of honor.

"Tim honey what on earth is the occasion?" she whispered to him.

"It's Marcello's birthday!" Tim whispered quickly. Oriana's mouth fell wide open.

"Oh my God!? It is my son's birthday!" Oriana shouted out with excitement.

He didn't say anything, but nodded with confirmation.

"I'm so sorry darling!" she said quickly touching Marcello's arm. "I was so caught up with work that I forgot your birthday! Would you forgive mommy?" Oriana said feeling guilty.

"That's OK mommy!" Marcello said innocently.

"Well this is certainly a first time for me!" She remarked, as she embraced Marcello and kissed him lovingly.

"Did you thank Tim for his surprise?" Oriana asked her son.

"Thank you Tim," Marcello responded bashfully.

"You'll get your gifts later at home! This is a special Persian restaurant! I ate with my parents here a few times, a long time ago! I hope it will be a special place for you to remember too!" Tim explained to Marcello.

On the way back home, Oriana sat on the passenger seat allowing Tim to drive her car. Marcello was in the back looking around, enjoying the sun.

"A Torture Club!" Tim sneered, passing by an advertisement sign.

"What's that?" she asked, not familiar with Hollywood advertising posters.

"The Torture Club?" Tim repeated, looking at her.

"It's a place for psycho sexual patients!" Tim answered, annoyed with the poster.

"You mean there are patients who get sexually treated there?" She asked with a shock on her face.

"I think the word is 'sexually satisfied,'" Tim remarked.

"You mean people find satisfaction in being tortured?" She asked not believing such club could exist in Hollywood.

"Yes, so they say." Tim replied, keeping his eyes on the road.

"Oh, my god! Fortunately, we don't have that problem!" She remarked, as she kissed him.

"Look Marcello a ferris wheel there! Would you like to ride on it?" Tim asked, with a quick glance on the boy.

"Yes please!" Marcello responded happily.

After Tim parked the car in the parking structure, he purchased some tickets to the City Fair. It was a chance for paparazzi to take some pictures. Even some customers at the carnival recognize the trio asking for their autographs. They enjoyed riding on whirl-around, eating pizza ,and the animal show. She realized, this was probably one of the happiest times of her life. Happiness is like good health, often isn't really appreciated until it's gone!

Just a few months ago, she was miserable while living with her mom and grandpa in Italy. Now, although she had lost father of her child, she had gained a wonderful friend and a great lover. Ever since she arrived to Los Angeles, Tim has always been there for her. Having fans all over the world who loved her wasn't enough! Being the Naples Goddess in Italy didn't matter to her unless she was with him. She may loose her fans and they could all desert her, but someone like Tim would be her rock to lean on! He was a amazing man, and she was so lucky to have him in her life.

They left the City Fair right after lunch. Marcello was tired as they drove home, he fell asleep in the back seat.

"I know this area, would you like me to show you around?" Tim asked, driving through the city.

"Sure," She replied, not having a care in the world.

The Santa Yens Mountains rose on the east, on the right, and the ocean was on the left. It was a spectacular contrast to the shore. They were silhouetted against the blue sky and white clouds. Santa Barbara had one of the most beautiful views on the West Coast.

"It seems like paradise. I have never seen such a nice view in my life! It's amazing!" Oriana remarked.

"Santa Barbara is a beautiful place and has a different look than any other cities. This city does not separate itself between the rich and poor, rather the rich are separated from the rich. The rich people in the foothills have tree-lined driveways and caverns, which could be mistaken for national parks. These were the estates of the Midwestern families marring each other, to continue the lineage." Tim explained, increasing Oriana's information on the city.

The sun was setting down on the ocean as Tim parked the car on a scenic view. They watched the sun set on the ocean's horizon. The night was dark and chilly, when they arrived home. Tim picked up the sleepy boy out of the car, and took him inside his bedroom. Ellie stopped by their house for few minutes.

"Hi guys! Did you have a great day?" she asked with a smile.

"Yes how about you?" Answered Oriana, inviting her in.

"Very, very busy the whole day! Can we talk for a minute?" Ellie asked, having something on her mind.

"Sure." Oriana replied, as Tim came back to living room. They looked at her curiously.

"OK let me open up and be honest with you! Since this morning, I have been busy looking into the film budget. I have paid bills, and done some calculations. According to the numbers, the spending has exceeded the budget, and I may have to resort bankruptcy which would stop the filming of our movie! If I'm not able to get a loan from any bank to finish production of our film, I don't know what to do!" Ellie remarked with big concern for the film.

"Ellie, we understand your concern and are ready to help you however we can!" Tim replied with sympathy.

"Thank you for your understanding Tim. Unfortunately, I'm way over budget and I know you can't help! If I could figure something out, we can continue filming, otherwise I have to shut down the production!" Ellie remarked sadly.

• • •

The telephone rang at 2:30am. Oriana woke up looking at the clock before she picked it up.

"Hello!" She mumbled into the receiver, rubbing her eyes.

"This is Dr. Baz! I'm calling from the hospital in Naples, Italy, on behalf of your grandfather Senior Phillipo Rousliny! Sorry if I woke you up!" The voice was warm and comforting. Oriana sat up right on the bed.

"Is something wrong with my grandfather Dr. Baz?" She asked cautiously.

"No." Dr. Baz replied.

"Then what? Is he dead?" Oriana asked in confusion.

"No, he is not dead Oriana! I want you to honor his wish and come back to Naples soon to see him! It is very important that you do that! Chow for now!" Dr. Baz conveyed his news.

She didn't know what to think of that phone call when she hung up the phone. Was there something wrong with his grandfather that Dr. Baz wasn't telling her! She began crying.

"What happened?" Tim asked, sitting on the bed next to her.

"My Grandfather Rousliny is in the hospital! Probably he had a heart attack! His doctor wants me and Marcello to go back to see him!" She replied sadly.

"It's okay honey. Ellie has to temporary shut down the film production and you..." Tim remarked, trying to simplify the matters but she interrupted.

"I can't leave without you!" Oriana said desperately.

"It's okay. You'll see..." Tim assured her.

"I want you to come with me to Italy!" Oriana said quickly.

"Let's talk it over with Ellie then we decide!" He responded trying to calm her down.

9

Producer

Naples, Italy

THE LONG PAN AMERICAN jumbo jet departed Los Angeles International Airport, to Rome, Italy. During the flight, Oriana explained her family story and back ground to her boyfriend Tim. She was a short brown dress and a expensive pair of glasses, hiding her worried eyes behind it's dark lenses. She exited the airplane while holding her son's hand on one side, and Tim's hand from the other side. A lot of people were gathered at the airport to greet her. The airport security officers escorted them to a private waiting pavilion. Tim went through the immigration process, while reporters and paparazzi crowded outside waiting for them.

In a short interview with a popular TV station in Rome, Oriana indicated that she returned to visit her family. She mentioned about her film production in Hollywood, and that she was the star who played the role of Joan of Arc. Her thoughts were focused more on her Grandpa in the hospital. Her mom Gina greeted them with open arms. She hugged her daughter and grandson Marcello, and gave a warm welcome to Tim. Oriana introduced him to her mother Gina formally, while a large limo waited for them outside the terminal.

Airport security guarded them from the media when they exited the airport. They were escorted to Naples, by two police motorcycle cops and cars. Behind them, the photographers and news media followed. Oriana knew they were the hottest news on the Italian television and every newspapers. A picture of her would worth thousands of dollars, and everyone was out there to snap that shot!

Philipo Rousliny was on the upper echelon of films, as a great directors in Italy. He was in competition with other directors such as Carlo Ponti, and Vittorio De Sica. In the tragic years after World War II, the land was extremely cheap in Italy, and Rousliny took advantage of the time to invest into farmland, and historical buildings to renovate them. On one occasion, he came across with a property which was atop a hill. It was roughly on five acres of land. He fell in love with it and purchased it. In honor of his beloved wife, he named it "Lucretia". The land stretched on the hill with vineyards. Giving him a chance to find a new passion in life, making wine.

Later on he remodeled the property to make it a beautiful mansion. He was extremely proud of it. A two story mansion with ten bedrooms, seven baths and great view of the hills. All the main rooms opened onto broad verandas with flower-filled beds, and cypress-bordered walks, which led to a dozen different hidden gardens with fountains.

Upon arrival to the mansion, the beautiful black gate opened up for the limo. The gate was closed, leaving the news media away from the home. Once inside the mansion, Tim was so impressed with the huge Italian furniture, massive carved sofas, high-backed dining room chairs, the mahogany armoires, floor covered Persian rugs, a few fireplaces, ceramic tiles, and chandeliers hanging from the ceiling. He has never seen a Italian mansion with so much history to it before!

Oriana recalled her childhood there living with her mom and Grandpa. It seemed like a long time ago! Marcello was too young too remember, and lots have happened since that time. Walking to the kitchen, Oriana found their family cook, Susie.

"Susie! How are you?" she asked, almost lifting her up as she hugged her.

"Oriana, I'm so glad to see you again! You've changed completely!" the tiny woman replied in her Italian accent.

They were shown to their bedrooms as Gina made preparation to visit the hospital. Oriana could hardly wait to see her grandfather Philipo.

At age 78, Philipo Rousliny was a tall man with broad shoulders. He had tanned skin, thick fierce eyebrows, and thick gray hair. Below his aquiline nose, there was his firm jaw. Around the vineyard, he would wear a long sleeve shirt to cover his body, and a straw hat to keep the sun away.

It was a one hour ride to the hospital. The limousine had dark tinted windows, making it impossible to recognize anyone inside. Once inside the hospital, they were directed to the critical care unit. Outside the room Tim waited, while Oriana, Gina, and Marcello went inside. She gazed at the pale figure lying on the bed! Oriana was shocked at how much her grandpa had changed in such a short time. Something about him suggested pain and unhappiness in his eyes.

Gently she kissed his cheek and held his hands. He opened his eyes affectionately, and looked at his granddaughter. He was glad to see her and for the last time, gather his family around him. It brought so much pride, and joy to him before he died.

"Oriana, I'm so glad to see you again! You resemble your grandmother a lot, and remind me of her! You are one of the rare women in the movies, and will be successful in life. I have put my whole estate and will under your name. When I die, they will be all yours. Make me proud my dear! I love you dearly!"

"Grandpa, you taught me everything I know. I promise to protect all your estate and bring pride to our family. I will make you proud!" Oriana replied, reassuring her grandfather. She held his hand for a moment, and placed a kiss on his cheek, while tears ran down from her eyes. Her grandfather's eyes closed slowly, and forever.

A few hours after her grandfather's passing, the TV stations and newspapers broke the news. They wanted the whole world to know about a big loss in Italy! They wanted Oriana to make a statement about her grandpa's death, but she remained in mourning. One of the TV stations covering the story indicated that, "the greatest director of all time, Rousliny had passed at age 78, only a few hours ago." Other related stories covered his life, and how successful he was at film making. The reporters interviewed celebrities, writers, movie stars, church officials, and ordinary people. They expressed their sorrow, and spoke highly of Rousliny and his devotion to his family and career. Most people guessed, that Oriana had already inherited his estate including the mansion with the vineyard worth millions.

The memorial service and burial for Philipo Rousliny was held at one of the most famous cathedrals in Naples. Superstars, celebrities and Italian society came to pay their respects. Wreaths of flowers came in from charity organizations, and the government officials. He was being buried in a special casket in the cemetery.

At the burial services, Oriana stood next to her mother. She wore a black dress and hat, with dark glasses. Her mother also wore a black suit. Standing behind them, Tim and Marcello were next to each other. Tim was holding his hand, they were dressed in black suit as well. After the ceremony, each person approached and place a red rose over the casket. The reporters were present and covering the story moment by moment. They wondered about the mysterious American gentleman with Oriana. Some said, he was her bodyguard!

A few days later, Rousliny lawyer's office called them to review the will. A group of people including Oriana, Gina, Tim and Marcello, along with representatives from charities and churches, who expected to receive donations from his estate. They were anxious, and uneasy sitting around a table, as the attorney opened the envelopes containing the will. Oriana was very calm, and seemingly indifferent. A small chest was opened by a key, as th attorney took some other sealed envelopes out of it. He read the will as follows:

"All the proprietorship rights, movable or not movable, chattels and real estate, studio, and movies are given; (one part) to Gina and Oriana, another (one part) to churches and charities, and (two parts) to Oriana and her son Marcello."

This division of assets annoyed the representatives. They signed the documents, and left the attorney's office immediately. Oriana asked her mom to watch over Marcello, while they looked over the documents and discussed them with the attorneys. The documents covered were; the Lucretia mansion, all his stocks, and cash money in the banks. The attorney's indicated the amount, and documents necessary to access the funds.

It was a long day as they returned back to the mansion. Outside air was fresh, and temperature was around mid 70's. After dinner they went into the night air, outside on the deck. Sitting on the patio chairs, they looked at the panoramic view of the land and the vineyard.

"I don't know what to do! I don't want to leave you!" She said sadly.

He cradled her in his arm, lost in his own thoughts. Now, he realized what kind of power she had over him. He was all she knew about generosity and paternal warmth. Tim was worried where her destiny was taking her! They both stayed in silence without exchanging any words.

• • •

One week past her grandfather's funeral, Oriana received a call from a the studio's office. His grandfather's secretary, Loretta requested a meeting. They agreed and the next day, a limo picked them up from the mansion. Oriana knew every corner of the studio. Once the limo pulled up in front the office, the paparazzi were expecting their arrival. They snapped pictures, as the limousine's door opened up.

Loretta was a 65 years old woman, dressed in a black and gray suit. She greeted, and welcomed them both with friendly smile. She expressed her condolences to Oriana, for her grandfather's passing. Having been in the filming business for the past thirty years, she knew all the movie stars, celebrities, and other directors, inside and outside of Italy. She had known Oriana as a child star for years, and loved her.

"You are the most beautiful girl in the world!" Loretta said without any hesitation.

"Am I?" Oriana asked jokingly.

"Yes you are! Your beauty is in the same caliber as well known movie star as Sophia Loren, Gina your mother!" Loretta said seriously.

"Thank you Loretta." Oriana responded modestly.

"When a man looks at you, he sees something which he has never seen before! They can only dream, or see it on the movie screen, but not in reality! Most men are terrified to talk to you, because they think they don't have anything to offer you! You will always be a super star! All beautiful women suffer from the same problem. It takes a special man to understand your kind!" She remarked, as she was speaking to her own daughter.

"Thanks for your warm heart and great advice." Oriana replied affectionately.

"One day when you are together, rich and famous, tell everyone that I was right in my predictions!" she remarked as she looked at Tim.

"Let me get back to our work at hand! I had a call from your grandfather's attorney yesterday. They explained, and our office is aware of your new film in Hollywood. We are very glad of your production's progress on the Joan of Arc film, and based on what we have read in the newspaper's articles, this movie would be a Oscar wining film!" Loretta explained, as she directed them to her boss's office.

When they entered into her grandfather's office, there was a large mahogany desk in the corner of the room. There were a few phones on his desk, and a desk light. The empty space between the desk's legs, brought back some childhood memories for Oriana as she began to cry uncontrollably. Tim and Loretta went to her side to comfort her.

She was five years old, when her grandpa brought her to his

office. It was her first time there. She used to watch the films while he was working in this office. Oriana hid under his desk one time, when she ran away from her mom Gina. Her mom asked her to come out, and not to bother her grandpa. She came out, her grandpa gave her one paper and colored pencils to draw pictures.

"Honey, are you OK? I know this room brings back a lot of memories for you. Take it easy!" Loretta remarked, handing her over a tissue to wipe her tears.

"Would you like to see the studio?" Oriana asked Tim with affection.

"No honey. It's not necessary, because it reminds you of the past," Tim replied.

In the absent of her grandpa from the studios, a management team where chosen to carry on the daily work responsibilities, and provide a weekly and monthly report for her review. Oriana wasn't happy with that arrangement. In fact, Loretta had taken too many responsibilities, and had stretched herself too thin at the studio. Oriana felt a great sympathy for her, seeing how complicated her responsibilities were.

"Tim darling, we need to talk about our future plans!" she said, as they were sitting inside the limousine, returning back to the mansion. After dinner they went out on the terrace. The comfortable armchairs was inviting to sit down for a glass of wine. Oriana poured a glass of wine, and sat down on his lap.

"Are you worried?" He asked.

"Uh-huh," She replied.

"About us?" He gathered.

"Uh-huh," She nodded.

"Okay, promise me one thing," he said without hesitation.

"Hmmm?" she looked at him.

"You have to stop worrying, and learn to trust me. Tell me, what's bothering you?" he asked, wanting to get to the source of the problem.

"Everything here, including you!" She replied quickly.

"Me?" he asked puzzled.

"Yes you! Since my grandfather died, I have so many responsibilities here in Naples, and don't know how to deal with them. I

don't want to lose you, or have to chose between you and.............
You have to help me!" she explained in confusion.

"Which one is most important to you?" Tim asked calmly.

"I love you and want to be with you! I want us to finish filming in Hollywood too! The studio here in Naples can be managed by Loretta." she remarked.

"OK honey. What can you do to help Ellie?" he asked not sure where Oriana was going with her thoughts.

"I can give her a loan to finish production of the film!" she replied quickly.

"I think that's a great idea. Have your attorney draw up legal papers, after you talk to Ellie! You can give her the good news!" Tim answered with excitement.

"Great! Now, how do I deal with you?" she said playfully.

"Well, anything you like! Let me see if I could help you a little….." He replied, kissing her.

He lifted her up from his lap, and carried her into their bedroom. As he undressed her, she covered him with hasty kisses. She felt his hands on her naked body searching for her pleasure spots. She moaned at loud with pleasure as his figures found her G-spot. "Oh…..yeah!!"

To add more pleasure, his mouth captured every sweet essence of her body. She released a louder sigh, as she came! Drowned in sweat pleasure of their oral love making, she felt satisfied! Her body was relaxed. They fell asleep into each other's arms while spooning each other on the bed.

10

The Agreement

Santa Barbara

BACK IN LOS ANGELES, Ellie Mitchell felt invigorated. She had to find a way to gather more money to fund the rest of the production of her film, Joan of Arc. She wasn't able to get her funding from a bank, and her last resort was her husband's best friend Mike Grant. She called his office.

"Hi, may I talk with Mr. Grant?" Ellie asked his secretary.

"Who's calling please?" She asked robotically.

"A friend." Ellie replied.

"Could I have your name please?" secretary persisted.

"Ellie Mitchell." She replied unwillingly.

"I'll see if Mr. Grant is available!" She replied.

"I'm sure he'll be available to me!" Ellie remarked.

"Let me check please. One moment!" the secretary responded politely.

"Mr. Grant is in conference, and asked not to be disturbed!" She stated returning back on the line, after a short wait

"Please tell him, this is regarding an important matter. I insist that you connect me immediately!" Ellie demanded quickly.

"Please hold!" she replied, when she put the line on hold.

"What's going on Ellie? I heard you stopped production on Joan of Arc! Did you forget about our deal?" Mike asked rudely, when he came on the line.

"What deal?" Ellie responded, acting like she didn't know what he was talking about.

"I've been anxiously waiting for your call!" Mike replied impatiently.

"Oh, yes! You mean my body?" Ellie responded with anger in her voice.

"Just you and me! How about dinner tonight?" Mike ignored her remark.

"Good point!" Ellie replied annoyed with him.

"You didn't answer yet," Mike persisted.

"So, do you want my answer? Go to hell!" she yelled at him on the phone, when she slammed the phone down.

It was a hot summer night. Mike tried to call Ellie's home in Santa Barbara, CA several times, but Ellie didn't pick up the phone. Around1:30am her cell phone rang. She woke up from a deep sleep, thinking it was him calling again.

"Damn you, Mike!" Ellie answered her cell phone angrily.

"Ellie…it's me…Oriana." Oriana replied on the other line.

"Oriana! I'm so sorry, I thought you were someone else!! I heard about your grandfather's death, and meant to call you earlier to express my condolences. How are you?" Ellie replied feeling guilty.

"Everything is fine! Were you trying to get a loan from Mike Grant?" Oriana asked curiously.

"Yes, but that didn't work out!" Ellie replied with disappointment.

"How about other banks?" Oriana asked quickly.

"Nothing! I can't get a loan!" Ellie said with frustration.

"OK then! I have some good news for you!" Oriana said happily.

"I'm listening." Ellie replied, glued to her phone.

"I can lend you a loan!" Oriana said with excitement.

"Oriana, are you serious?" Ellie asked in disbelief.

"Yes very serious!" Oriana exclaimed.

"How much can you lend me?" Ellie asked, now standing up from her bed.

"There are some conditions but we'll talk about that later!" Oriana said, like a businesswoman.

"Of course! What are they?" Ellie responded, now pacing the floor back and forth.

"I'll have our attorney draw up an agreement. We can talk about it, when we return back to L.A!" Oriana remarked with joy.

"Thank you so much! This was the best news I got all day! I'll wait for your return, and get together later. Good night Oriana." Ellie replied, thinking her problems are all over.

• • •

The Los Angeles Times had a big headline on their cover page. It stated, "Panther movie mogul was arrested on embezzlement charges. Mike Grant, the head executive of Panther Movie Industry had been arrested, and taken to jail. He is waiting for a hearing, and the bail is set for one million dollars."

Justice was served! Ellie Mitchell was pleased to hear that news. She didn't care for his sex advances. Knowing he was her husband's best friend, made her feel sorry for him.

The departure time to Los Angeles, California, was nearing. The two weeks trip to Naples, Italy finally ended. They had to say goodbye to her mother Gina and Loretta, and catch their flight. Once again with her son and favorite man on her side, they were headed for U.S. This time it was different; she was wealthy, madly in love with a charming man who adored her, and an international movie star!

They held hands as the airplane soared into the night sky.

Marcello fell asleep quickly after dinner. It gave an opportunity for Tim and Oriana to have a little conversation with each other.

"Why is the distribution of Joan of Arc in Europe a condition? What's so important to you?" Tim asked, starting the conversation.

"Because Joan of Arc is a French hero who is well known in Italy!" Oriana replied calmly.

"I agree with you. Don't you think Ellie knows that too?" Tim asked, not understanding Oriana's point.

"I'm not sure, if she does!" Oriana replied casually.

"I'm so proud of you honey!" Tim remarked with a smile.

"Proud of me? For what?" She asked playfully.

"I'm proud of you because you have become a movie producer!" Tim replied with amazement.

"Thank you honey." She responded, with a kiss on his lips.

The airplane touched down in Los Angeles airport. They got a taxi cab ride to Malibu, as the housekeeper welcomed them home. She helped them unpack their luggage as Tim went to his home office checking on mail.

"Would it be possible housekeeping for us more hours weekly?" Oriana asked the housekeeper.

"Yes Madam. I have no family in this city. Mr. Forist only needed me part-time housekeeping, but I can work full time if necessary." The housekeeper responded happily.

"Ok then, you are hired to work full time starting immediately. I need you to take care of my son Marcello. Do you have any questions?" Oriana asked, trying to make household arrangements

"No Madam thank you." The housekeeper replied.

"I have great news for you!" Tim said as he walked back to living room.

"What is it?" She asked.

"Before we sign an agreement with Ellie, I have asked one of my friends to look over the contract. He is a skillful attorney. His name is Bill Craft. We went to high school together, and played college football. He is the most distinguished attorney in the Hollywood. He has agreed to meet us tomorrow night." Tim remarked making sure the agreement was drawn correctly.

"Thanks honey. What would I do without you!" she replied, knowing he was there for her.

Bill was a handsome black man, remarkably fit with thick short hair. He was athletically built, around thirty five years. His appearance, and confidence was intimidating to a lot of people, but not to Tim. He had built an empire, based on his knowledge and sense of power. All his investments were profitable and successful. He was married once, but no children. His wife passed away from breast cancer a few years back, while he remained mentally and emotionally devoted to the memory of his wife. He choose not to date any other woman again.

The following night, after they had dinner, the doorbell rang. Tim welcomed Bill in the house, and introduced him to Oriana. The three of them walked to the patio and had some wine. They were enjoying their time together as Bill asked questions. He learned about Oriana's life story, and their relationship together. At some point in their conversations, Bill offered to look over the agreement drawn up by the Italian attorney. The contract agreement was drawn up between Oriana, and Ellie Mitchell as a loan to complete filming of Joan of Ark. Bill agreed to represent her, in facilitating to transfer money from Italy, and over see the loan given to Ellie Mitchell. They signed the contract and Bill said goodbye.

It took a week before Bill was able to transfer some money from Italy to U.S. Ellie was waiting impatiently to be contacted by him. A few days after, Bill called Ellie to meet up. Oriana and Tim accompanied Bill and formally introduced him to Ellie

"I'm glad to meet you Bill," Ellie said while shaking Bill's hand.

"Thank you Ellie. I hope this meeting will be successful for all of us," Bill said sincerely.

The attorneys began explaining, and negotiating the terms of the contract for their clients. Tim was sitting quietly, watching all interactions. They were unable to come to any agreement immediately, and ended the meeting in good terms.

"I want to say something!" Tim said urgently before they got up to leave. Oriana and Bill looked at each other in puzzle.

"The purpose of this meeting was to come into a meeting of the minds. On one hand, Ellie needs to get a loan to finish filming of Joan of Arc. In this recession, she has not been able to obtain that loan anywhere! On the other hand, Oriana has inherited her grandfather's estate, and is willing to offer her a loan. This is the financial backing which would help the production to move forward. Ellie is our friend and we want to help!"

Everyone in the room nodded their head in agreement, and verbally agreed to sign all documents. Tim's common sense approach worked well, and everyone seemed to be excited to move forward.

A week later the production of the film began again. They were so close to wrap up the movie, therefore everyone was under a lot of stress for compressed shooting schedules. They had fallen behind the schedule, and it was time to catch up with it fast. The stressful time adjustments had affected Oriana greatly. As Joan of Arc, she had larger parts to prepare for and memorize more lines. She had worked longer hours to make the scene successful, but she was unhappy because it took away from her personal life! She was so exhausted by the time she got home, and didn't get to see Tim and Marcello that much. Through it all, Tim remained at her side and supportive.

It was early in the morning, when Oriana left. Tim was still in bed sleep. He woke up when the front door closed, and got up to take a shower. Looking in the mirror, he saw his own reflection. A handsome thirty-five-year-old man who stayed in shape, and was athletically fit. He flexed his arms to see the definition on his muscles. Thankfully they looked good. Changing his mind to take the shower, he decided to do a quick run on the beach.

It was a early morning and the fog got thicker coming from the ocean. He continued running, until he heard a voice urging him to stop! His vision was obscured, as he couldn't tell how far he had run.

"Who are you?" The giant body asked.

"A passerby! Who are you?" Tim asked, without expecting anyone asking him that.

"This is a restricted area sir! You need to return back!" The man ordered, as he got closer.

"This is a public beach, and I have every right to run or walk around it! Who are you?" Tim asked irritated.

"I'm Big John, a security guard to a famous director here. He lives in this villa!" He responded as if he was in control.

"Sorry, my name is Tim Forist. I'm an actor," Tim replied to the man.

"I have heard of you! You are the actor in 'Joan of Arc' film?" The giant man stated with excitement.

"Yes I am!" Tim said in amusement as he began running back toward home.

11

Reconciliation

LATE IN THE AFTERNOON, Ellie walked around impatient-ly. Holding a cup of coffee in her hand, thinking and pacing the floor repeatedly. Her heart was racing fast, as she thought at any moment it would pop out of her body! Nervous and stressed out, it was hard to believe that her husband Greg had call her, the night before. He cried on the phone apologizing! He said, "I'm sorry for what I've done to you! I will take full responsibility for my actions! Please forgive me and give me another chance!" He wanted to see her in person to personally apologize from her! She accepted, but did not wish to discuss things over the phone.

Over the past few months of separation, Ellie had heard from their mutual friends that Greg had stopped seeing other women. In the past several weeks, Ellie had seen a psychiatrist who told her not to see Greg, until she was completely ready. She had a hard time sleeping and had lost her appetite to eat food. Ellie felt lonely and depressed. She wanted to be loved and cherished by her husband again. That's why she accepted Greg's apology! She believed that things would get better between them, and her life would go back to normal again.

There was a knock on the door. Her heart began to beat faster, as she opened the door. Greg was standing there with flowers in his hand.

"Ellie my darling, please accept my apology! Please forgive me!" Greg said sincerely.

He embraced and kissed her. They both had tears running from their eyes, but Ellie remained quiet letting Greg continue with his apology.

"I was a fool cheating on you! I'm so sorry that I lied to you, and hurt you! It was a big mistake! I messed up our lives, and I'm sorry for what I have done! Please give me a chance to make it all right again! Would you forgive me darling?" Greg continued on showing his pain and sorrow on his face. It was coming from his heart, It wasn't a shallow apology!

"It doesn't matter!" Ellie responded quickly.

"But it does to me Ellie!" Greg remarked innocently.

"OK then, I accept your apology! You must promise me that you would never do that again!" She said firmly.

"I promise you darling, that I will never hurt you again!" He replied emotionally.

Satisfied with her personal life going to the right direction, Ellie had to focus more efforts into promoting the film. She had to update their progress in filming, as they were so close to wrapping up the movie. She called up all news media, and television reporters. It was arranged for a news conference the following day at the film's location.

She took a deep breath by the microphone, and began speaking about their latest production progress. The reporters loved the story about her production had to shut down due to the shortage of funds, and how destiny changed the course of her life, when Oriana inherited a new empire and giving her a loan to finish filming. The press couldn't hardly wait to reveal that to the public, a story with happy ending!

The cast of Joan of Arc film were working hard to wrap up

things with the production. Ellie was supervising the edit of all takes, and staying on top of her budget at the end of the day. It made her happy that they were on the right track. Oriana was working long hours as well, she had to practice the stunt moves for the next day shooting. Leaving her movie trailer one night, she caught up with Ellie going home. Ellie accepted to give her a ride home.

"We had such a wonderful day today!" Ellie said driving the car.

"Yes we did but I'm so tired. I can picture myself relaxing in a hot bathtub with a glass of wine," Oriana replied, leaning her chair back.

"You know, most movie stars have a stunt doubles, I don't understand why you don't use a stunt woman in your scenes?" Ellie remarked, concerned for her.

"You are right but I prefer doing the stunts myself! Don't worry, I know how to take care of myself," Oriana replied with her eyes closed.

"You know I worry about you! Let me change the subject! How long have you been dating Tim?" Ellie asked curiously.

"Close to four months now. Why?" Oriana asked opening her eyes.

"No particular reason! He is such a perfect gentleman and has a great personality. My common sense tells me that he is in love with you!" Ellie said from her observations.

"Wow, I'm amazed how well your common sense works Ellie! He has done so much for me and Marcello and I can't ever repay him." Oriana said honestly.

"I wish you the best, and hope some day you marry him. Let me give you a few golden rules to remember! (1) Find the most amazing thing you can find about your man and compliment him on it all the time! Something that you know, he is the most proud of. It could be anything or even his body parts such as; his eyes, hair, smile, or even part of his body. (2) When you are in bed together, tell him he is the most sensational lover that you ever had! (3) Always admire him for his sense of knowledge and assure him that he is the smartest man that you know! With these three golden rules, you'll succeed in life!" Ellie advised her as a good friend.

"Thanks honey. I appreciate it sharing them with me." Oriana replied.

"Oh, I forgot to tell you something! We are invited to a friend's party tomorrow night. You and Tim are invited to go as well." Ellie remarked casually.

"We love to go, except Tim and I don't know anyone else there!" Oriana responded, as they arrived in front of Tim's place.

"Oh, don't worry! The party is a celebration of my husband and I getting back together again! For a while, we have been separated from each other, because he cheated on me with another woman! He has apologized and admitted to his wrong doings. I have decided to forgive him, and start our new life together." Ellie said with a smile.

"Well in that case, let me talk to Tim about it and get back to you." Oriana replied saying goodnight.

"Hi honey I'm home!" She said at loud once she entered the house. Placing her purse on the chair nearby, she waited for Tim to say something. Shortly after, he walked in and greeted her.

"I missed you honey!" He said holding her in his strong arms.

"I missed you too honey." She said placing a kiss on his lips.

"How are you doing honey? You must be tired!" he asked her with sympathy.

"I'm OK but very tired honey, it's been a long day." Oriana replied, still in his arms.

"Let me get you a glass of wine, then fix you a nice relaxing hot bathtub! How does that sound to you?" Tim said trying to make her feel comfortable.

"That sounds great honey." She replied.

"Just relax right here, I get you some wine. How was your day?". Tim asked, while picking up a bottle of wine. He poured it into a glass and walked toward her.

"I was busy practicing the movie stunts for the next shot tomorrow. Fortunately, all the fighting scenes are over and the story line would be focusing more on your role!" she remarked as she drank her wine.

He sat next to her on the couch and she wrapped her arms around his neck. A little soft kiss on his lips, triggered a great respond from him. Moving his hand up to her breasts, he held them into his hands. She closed her eyes, as he kissed her neck, shoulders and worked his lips down to where he cupped her breasts. She started to make sounds of ecstasy as he cautiously picked her up, and walked to his bedroom. Her breathing grew rapid, as he took her clothes off. She reached out to him, unbuckling his belt and unzipping his pants. His passion rose as he unleashed his wild and uncontrollable desire for her. She fondled him as his heart beat pondered against his chest. His body went limp on top of hers. Their breathing slowly synchronized as their love making made them reach orgasm together.

• • •

It was late afternoon the following day, when Oriana and Tim got ready for Ellie's party. Early in the day, Marcello spent some quality time with his mom walking around the beach and picking up sea shells. They were happy to do some bike riding, and play catch with Tim. Oriana kissed him and said she had to get ready for the party. The housekeeper was aware that they were going to a party later that night.

Walking out of the bedroom, they both looked splendid. Tim was wearing a handsome summer suit, and Oriana had a beautiful white short dress. The back of her dress was cut low, in a shape of a heart. Her soft beautiful back looked flawless, resembling a Venous statue! The dress was tailored specially for her compact and superb body. She accessorized the dress with a very expensive diamonds necklace and earrings. Her grandfather gave her the diamond jewelry. They were from Naples, Italy.

Oriana smiled at him as they advanced toward the door. "Honey you look like a goddess!" Tim managed to say.

On the way to the party, Ellie dropped by to pick them up. She drove the car to the villa. It was a circle drive, and Ellie drove by the front door. There were many cars parked there already. Tim recognized the bodyguard. He was the man on the beach, which he ran into a week ago, while running. He was Greg Sight's bodyguard!

Greg maneuvered warmly toward his wife Ellie.

"These are my friends, Oriana Rousliny and Tim Forist." Ellie made the first introductions.

"It's so nice to meet you both. I have heard a lot about you!" Greg said, as he shock their hands.

"And.....this is my husband Greg Sight, " Ellie remarked proudly.

Greg was happy to meet all of them, specially his wife Ellie. He missed being with her. Gathering all their family and friends together, was the only way he could show how much she means to him! Oriana clung to Tim's arms as they walked toward the bar. A music band was playing in the background, and the guests were having a great time drinking, laughing, and renew their acquaintances.

"Darling, you look so beautiful tonight! I'm so happy we are back together again!" Greg said to his wife Ellie as he kissed her hand.

She felt great being among her friends again. There were local columnists, and some reporters there giving Ellie a chance to talk about her film. She did not wish to discuss her separation from Greg, or to put any focus on her personal life. She walked to the direction of Oriana and Tim at the bar. They looked like love birds, standing hand in hand and glowing with a visible aura of romantic excitements. Suddenly, Greg tried to get everyone's attention.

"May I have everyone's attention please!" Greg announced in the microphone.

"As you all know, tonight is a very special night! I want to publicly apologize from my lovely wife Ellie, and say how sorry I am making the mistakes! I want her to forgive me, and give me a chance to make it right this time! We have been separated for a while now, and I missed her dearly!" Greg remarked, standing in front of her looking into her eyes.

She was lost for words! All of the sudden, Greg knelt down

before her, took both her hands into his and kissed them. Strategically, he took out a small box from his pant's pocket. It was a beautiful, thick, white gold, diamond ring! He placed it gently on her ring finger, as Ellie's tears began to roll down on her face. She had him stand up, and put her arms around his neck.

"I accept your apology darling! I love you with all my heart," Ellie said emotionally looking at his eyes, then sealed it with a kiss.

The guests were happy to witness such special moment. They clapped their hands to show their support. It was a heart felt apology, and was done very well! Oriana and Tim congratulated both of them, and wished them, a wonderful new beginning in life. It was time to say goodbye.

• • •

Ellie and Greg were back together again, and everything seemed to be normal again. Laying in his arms gave her a feeling of love and sense of security. Like a ritualistic ballet, the movements of which only the two of them knew! Shifting from one position to another to rise the level of desire, from mountain top to the valley and back again to the peak of passion. Their hands were touching everywhere, and their movements fluid and beautiful. Times like this was impossible to live without him, she thought. For whatever it was, they felt right going through the emotion and make it beautiful. She didn't want their love making to end, she was burning with desires! It wasn't the act of love making that she loved, it was him and how he could make her feel!

The sun was shining through the window. Part of it was peaking through the curtains. Ellie could hear a bell ringing, and see the sun light. Quickly, she disentangled herself from Greg's arms, to check the clock.

"Oh my God! It's 10:15AM!" She said in disbelieve, leaping from the bed. She snatched a robe from the closet to cover her body.

"Honey, get up!" She said to Greg.

"What's wrong honey? What's the rush? It's Sunday!" Greg said with puzzle in his eyes.

"Oh Right! I forgot honey!," She said trying to relax.

"That's OK, come back to bed." He encouraged her.

"No honey, you didn't let me sleep last night!" She replied. He sat up leaning on his elbows.

"Are you going to stand there?" He persisted.

She stood there looking at him in the middle of the room. She was trying to make a decision. Seeing her hesitation Greg jumped up, and with one swift move he lifted her up from the ground. Ever so softly, he placed her on the bed and pressed against her body. Now, she was pinned down to bed under him, that's what he wanted!

"I love you honey, and I wouldn't ever let you go!" She whispered softly to him.

"I have a surprise for you!" He said, steering up some excitement in her.

"What is it honey?" She asked impatiently.

"You'll see! Let's go have breakfast now. I'm starving." He said, keeping her in suspension.

After the breakfast, he covered her eyes and guided her toward the beach side. There was a large yacht anchored there. It was right in front of the house, with two sailors on deck. They decorated the yacht beautifully. Slowly, and cautiously, Greg took her toward the deck. Quickly he uncovered her eyes, allowing her to digest what she was observing! She shouted happily and embraced him. To show her appreciation, she kissed him repeatedly all over his face as Greg gave her a tour of the yacht.

"I can't believe how beautiful this is! Thank you darling!" She remarked in disbelieve.

"This is for you honey! I wanted to make you happy, so I named it after you!" He replied honestly.

His cell phone rang! Greg had to step out of the yacht for a moment.

"Hello! Yes Marcus. What? There is a cancellation of our contract! Why? Are you kidding me?" Greg said as he hung up the cell phone angrily.

"What's wrong honey?" she asked her husband, seeing him upset.

"It was Marcus! He's a producer of a movie I was getting ready to direct. He just canceled the contract!" He explained angrily.

"I'm sorry honey, but you will find another movie to direct soon! I'm sure something will turn out!" Ellie assured him.

• • •

It was a nice sunny day, and Tim was playing a video game with Marcello. They were enjoying their time together, when the home phone rang suddenly. They both jumped up from the couch, when they heard Oriana scream. Running toward her to make sure she was ok, she was still talking on the phone.

"That's great news! We can be there in an hour!" She said, as she hung up the phone.

"Who was that honey?" Tim asked, not sure if Oriana was sad or happy.

"Oh that was Ellie! She invited us to go on her yacht! Hurry up you two, we're all going!" She remarked to Tim excitedly.

"She has a yacht? I didn't know that!" Tim said under his breath, hurrying to get ready quickly.

They drove Ellie's car back there. The security man John opened the door and greeted them, then they went toward the yacht. Marcello and Tim were dressed in white shorts and T-shirt. Oriana was wearing a beautiful sport dress with tennis shoes. She had a headband on and dark glasses.

They were welcomed by Ellie and Greg on board. Oriana was so excited to see the beautifully engraved name on the yacht. Ellie embraced her happily.

"This is a beautiful yacht!" Oriana said in amazement.

"I'm glad you like it. Ellie is crazy for it!" Greg replied.

"Let me give you a tour Oriana, come with me." Ellie remarked, as she walked toward the lower level. Greg was the captain wearing a Captain's hat. He skillfully steer the wheel around the Santa Barbara's coastline. Beside him, Tim sat with a glass of wine in his hand. They talked about politics, as Ellie and Oriana sat in the cabin below talking. Marcello curiously walked around aimlessly.

"What a nice surprise! Let's toast to your new beginning which will bring you two closer. To you, Ellie!" Oriana remarked, as they click their Champaign glasses together.

"This is also to my husband Greg. A great man and a fantastic lover. He is the best director in Hollywood, and I'm proud of him. Unfortunately, today he lost an opportunity to direct a film, but I believe, he is talented to direct our film! Therefore, I invited my husband to co-direct with me on Joan Of Arc!" Ellie remarked eagerly.

Oriana was speechless. Instead, she tried to enjoy her time on board. The sun was setting in the ocean, when the yacht dropped it's anchor. On the deck, Tim, Marcello, and Greg started to do some fishing. They were shocked to catch a few fish. The little boy had a big smile on his face as they got home.

• • •

The Local reporters had called Ellie's office to confirm the legitimacy of the news. She confirmed the news that Greg would be directing the second half of the film with her. It was interesting for reporters to know that Ellie's husband, a famous director would co-direct a film with his wife!

"I have to admit, my husband is one of the best directors in Hollywood! He is the right man for the job!" She responded, to one of the reporters.

Part of the story made the afternoon news. It covered the interview with Ellie, and made the national news. A few days later, the entertainment magazines had covered the scandals surrounding the film "Joan of Arc" in depth. Most people who were interviewed by reporters expressed their feelings, "We can't wait for the movie to come out." There were talk about the Oscars on this film, and a great chance for Oriana Rousliny win as the best actress!

It was time for Ellie to contact her niece Mary Fawcet. She was the manager of the Torture Club, and Ellie thought that the location may be a great place for filming of the prison scene on the movie. It was important for her to review the location prior to filming, and spend some time with Mary.

One day after the media coverage on TV, Ellie contacted Mary on her cell phone. Mary agreed to give her aunt a tour of the place.

Thinking ahead, she thought how famous they would be after the filming of Joan of Arc at their club. It would give them a national exposure and free advertising.

The Torture Club had many rooms. They were separated by iron divider walls and many antique equipments. There were torture tables, chains hanging on the walls and tables. In most rooms, they had single beds with white sheets in the corner, giving it an appearance of a small prison. Ellie was amazed at what she was witnessing. She told Mary that the atmosphere of the club was just perfect for their film! She had to make some adjustments to the rooms to make them look real. Remembering the end of the story, where Joan of Arc was captured by the soldiers, and was placed in the enemy's prison. She was hurt and tortured in the hands of the guards. "Yes this is the place to shoot the scene!" Ellie thought. She wondered if her husband would agree with her!

12

Capture and Trial

The wheel had to revolve, once the political party, for which she fought with such faith, would be ground into oblivion.

She was captured, as a prisoner in May 1430. English were proud, to have captured such great prize. Now, the English were determined, to put an end to her! They pressured the Duke of Burgundy, to turn her over. Joan didn't have any holy spirits or hear any voices while in prison. The last time, the holy spirits warned her about her approaching capture. The English paid ten thousand Franc, ransom to the Duke. Joan grew distraught, once she learned from her jailers, that she had been sold to the English.

One day, she found an opportunity. Without any hesitation, she threw herself out of the prison tower. It was seventy feet high. Hours later, the guards found her lying unconscious in a ditch. It was incredible, that she had survived. She wasn't even injured! She had been captured in the spring, as the summer was gone, then faded into autumn. All this time, King Charles had made no effort to pay her ransom to free her. He believed, that Joan had caused her own bad luck, by being too proud to take anyone's advice. So, it was easier for him to do nothing at all. It was politically important, from the English stand point, that her trial should not be thoroughly by her countrymen. So, they agreed in writing, that Joan should be kept a prisoner, under English supervision. If she was found guilty, she would be handed over, for public execution. During her time in the prison, the jailers gave Joan, ladies dresses to wear, but she never accepted them.

While Joan stayed a prisoner, at Duke Burgundy's castle tower, she was slowly moved to Rouen city, where her trial was going to take place. An English territory, almost 300 miles away. The journey was made in secrecy. If her friends were aware of her move, they would have mustered to save her. At some time on the journey, she was aware being near her friends. Though they were powerless, to make themselves known to her. It was around Christmas 1430, when Joan was arrived to the Rouen, second city in France. The same location, where Richard the Lionheart, had once been held captive.

Joan expected to be kept in a church prison, where she is guarded by priests and nuns. As it was customary in religious trials. Instead, the English put her in a dark cell in the castle of Rouen, where she was put in chains, and guarded by British soldiers. Where she prayed daily. She had no visitors, but only one from a doctor, who checked her to find out if she was a virgin!

• • •

A few days later, an agreement were drowned by Ellie's attorney between Ellie Mitchell and Mary Fawcet, as the manager of the Torture Club. Greg agreed that the location of the Club was the most suitable place for their filming. The crew were prepared to shoot the scene the next day.

In the story, Joan threw herself out of the prison tower into a ditch trying to escape. Greg was comfortable with the stunt woman doing the scene, since he had previously visited the set and met up with the stunt woman. It was planned for Oriana to stay in the bottom of the tower, and the stunt woman jump down from the high tower into the ditch.

It was a restless night for Oriana, and during the night she had nightmares at all hours of the morning. The next day, she woke up at 7:00 a.m. tired from lack of sleep. Tim had left home very early, driving to another location to shoot the scene on King Charles. Ellie was on location there expecting him. "A cold shower and some coffee would do me good!" thought Oriana to herself.

Once she turned off the shower, suddenly she felt like vomiting! The same feeling she had, when she was pregnant with Marcello! She brushed it off, drank a glass of milk and left to work. Arriving there on time, she walked quickly to her trailer. The make up artist was prepared for her, and she changed into her armor clothes. She was ready for her scene, and knew her lines. One check into the full length mirror, she looked ready for the final scenes! A production assistant knocked on the door.

"Are you ready, Oriana?" A crew members asked making sure she was ready.

"I'm ready!" she replied at loud.

"All set? You look terrific! How do you feel?" Greg asked, standing outside her trailer.

"I feel great and ready to take on whatever comes my way!" Oriana said with full confidence.

A huge air mattress was placed under the tower, where the stunt woman and Oriana had to jump into it.

"Ok everybody! Places please!" Greg shouted out. "Wait until I say "action" before you jump." Greg instructed the stunt woman and Oriana.

The camera men were ready. Greg shouted, "action!". The stunt woman jumped down from the tower, throwing herself onto the air mattress below, hidden from the camera. Within few seconds, Oriana threw herself onto the air mattress when suddenly she shouted.

"Oh my God, I'm bleeding!!" she said at loud terrified.

Instantly, Greg ran toward her concerned for her health.

"Get a doctor! Call an ambulance right away! She is bleeding badly!" He yelled at the crew.

Oriana was taken to the nearest hospital. Greg was unable to contact Tim, but called his wife to report in the incident. Tim and Ellie drove to the hospital from their location and rushed to the Emergency Room. Greg remained waiting in the hospital's reception area. Tim thought something had happened to Oriana on the set. He was disturbed and concerned for her safety.

The doctor came out of ER, and walked directly toward them.

"She will be OK, but she lost her baby!" The doctor remarked calmly..

"Were you aware of her pregnancy?" The doctor asked Tim calmly.

"No, I wasn't! May I see her now?" Tim asked impatiently.

"She has to rest for an hour at least before I let you see her!" The doctor explained.

It was a long one hour wait! Finally Tim was able to go into Oriana's room to visit her. She threw her arms around him and began weeping. Her tears wouldn't allow her to speak, and her hair was in disarray. He held her tight giving her courage to speak.

"It's OK honey. You will be alright soon. Tell me what happened?" Tim reassured her.

"This morning when I was taking a shower, I felt like throwing up. I didn't take it seriously because I was anxious to get to work. Everything was prepared for shooting and I didn't want to be late! Oh, I'm so sorry!" Oriana explained with disappointment.

"Honey, I'm sorry for the loss of the baby! I want you to get some rest and get better. Don't worry about the scenes, we are delaying the production until you get better!" Ellie said with concern as she hugged her.

"I'm so sorry! I'll get better in a few days." Oriana said, feeling guilty about the production being shut down.

"Don't worry honey, just focus on getting stronger and better." Tim said kissing her.

• • •

On February 21, 1431, Joan of Arc's faith was decided by two English judges. The judges were advised, by church law, to take her sentence lighter. After all, she was a nineteen year old peasant girl, who was unable to read or write, and didn't have a lawyer to help her.

It was a cold winter, around Christmas time. Joan was chained by the iron shackles to her feet, but the English cared less. She was watched around the clock, by five English soldiers, who were not chosen for their kindness. She was never free of their inquisitive eyes. She could walk the length of her prison cell, and never see outside. Sometimes, she lied down on her poor mattress, but seldom slept specially when she knew they were drunk. She prayed in silence, and dared not weep. Her safeguard against being rape, was her page's doublet and hose, to which she clung, days and nights. Though, the old black suit was worn thread bare at the knees, and elbows.

Her trial began in January 1431. To their surprise, it was discovered that this ignorant peasant girl, was not easily intimidated, and she was remarkable. She was clever, quick, bold, and saucy in answering the questions.

"I know nothing of the love or hate which God has for the English, but I do know that if the English had another hundred thousand soldiers, it would not help them take France! They will be driven out of France, and God will send victory to France over the English." Joan answered, to one of her questions, on the trial.

One time, the matrons of the city examined her, to prove beyond the reasonable doubt, that she was a virgin woman who was the only woman entered into that horrible cell! They sent her a gown to wear, but Joan flatly refused! The church, which judged her, allowed no priests to visit her, for daily communion with God.

There was no doubt, that she would be found guilty on the trial. Still, the trial was ruthless, and church officials spent weeks urging her to give up her false beliefs, and ask for forgiveness. Even with torture, Joan stood firm

"Why do you insist on dressing like a boy?" A judge asked her on the trial.

"It is for my safety, while living with male soldiers. Besides, my holly spirits commanded it!" she answered, without any hesitation.

Joan argued her case boldly. She insisted her holly spirits were heavenly. The judges were infuriated by her stubbornness. They led her to a torture chamber with its horrific screws, spikes and racks, to frighten and threatened her. Joan refused to accept the Church's views.

The holly spirits had assured her, that she should only answer boldly, during her three months trial. She believed , the spirits were sent from God, and did as she was told.

"I saw the spirits, with my own two eyes, as I see you! I believe in the existence of God!" She answered a question, another time.

She didn't make it easy for the English judges. Her clear, honest and candid replies, had left a heart felt mark, in the people who witnessed her testimony.

At the beginning of March 1431, she fell ill. Some said, it was food poisoning, caused by eating bad fish. In her weakness, she surrendered herself to death. She recovered quickly, but was growing weaker by confusion.

13

The Beginning of the End

Santa Barbara

AFTER A FEW DAYS of rest and recovery at home, Oriana was ready to return back to work again. She studied her lines and practiced her scenes in front of her mirror every day.

Thoughts were crossing her mind, as she practiced her lines. She compared her life living in Hollywood verses Italy. No doubt that Hollywood had dazzled and changed her life into a exotic and glamorous life style. Now, as a beautiful young Italian actress, she lived a graceful and hectic Hollywood life style!

Returning to the set of the film, she watched her stunt double playing the torture scene. It was interesting to see how similar their voices were together. Oriana played her part as Joan, when it was the trial scene. Greg had made her perform that act over and over, until she met his high standard of perfection.

Ellie was extremely happy with the production nearing it's end. Her husband's hard work as co-director was paying off well. A few weeks past, since Oriana lost her baby. Yet, she wouldn't discuss her inner feelings with anyone! She was hurt inside but Tim remained supportive of her. He helped out with Marcello and his school home work.

A cozy dinner for four was planned at the Mitchell's house. They have had a couple of rough weeks of filming the ending of the story. Now, it was time to relax and enjoy life a little. Oriana looked at her new blue dress hanging in the closet, and knew that's the dress she is wearing to the party. It's demur ruffled collar made her neck look slender, and the skirt was mid-length but short enough to show her extremely pretty legs. She put on a matching shoes and picked up her little purse and walked out of the room.

The door opened up and Marcello ran directly toward his mom. She opened her arms to embrace him. They were returning home from a toy store.

"Honey, I'm sorry we're late! Let me go change quickly, I'll be ready in five minutes!" Tim said, as she walked toward the master bedroom. Marcello brought his new toys and began showing them to his mom. He was so happy while describing how each game functioned.

It was seven o'clock when Tim pulled the Ferrari out of the garage. He opened the driver's door for Oriana, and she sat behind the wheel. He sat beside her on the passenger seat. It was a short drive to Greg's house but Oriana felt good driving the car. She pulled up in front of the door, and the security man John ran to welcome them.

"Honey you look magnificent tonight!" Tim complimented her as she held onto his arm.

"Thank you darling!" She replied with a smile.

"Wow, look at the two of you! The most handsome couple I know!" Ellie remarked as they walked in.

"Thanks honey! You look marvelous darling." Oriana responded.

"Come on in, let's have something to drink." Greg said directing them to the living room bar.

"I have a little surprise for you! After dinner I'll show you the edited version of the shooting we did a few days ago. I believe this is one of the best scenes we have shoot and Oriana was terrific!" Greg remarked, talking about the recent shooting.

"Honey, dinner is served on the terrace." Ellie said with a little humor.

The wooden terrace overlooked the city lights from one side, and the ocean from the other. The table was set romantically and elegantly. There was a enclosed glass terrace with many planters placed all around.

"It is very lovely," Oriana remarked pleasantly.

"I'm afraid we're used to it darling," Ellie replied eloquently.

When the dinner was over, they walked through the dining room toward a heavy wooden doors. Greg opened the door and they entered the room. Their eyes were wide open! Ellie could see the look of shock and disbelief in their faces! Tim let out a long low whistle.

"Wow! This is incredible!" He said with a look of amazement on his face.

The room was large and dimly lit. Three rows of oversized theatre chairs were set in the middle of the room in front of a movie screen. They were covered with heavy velour. Blending with the dark brown furniture, the walls were covered in a rich brown fabric. Approximately, 20 feet from the first row was a large movie screen. The room was designed like a mini movie theater!

"Wow, I don't know what to say! where should we sit?" Oriana asked still pleasantly shocked.

"Would you like front or back row?" Ellie asked nicely.

"Let me refresh all the drinks." Greg said, walking toward the wet bar in the room.

"No thanks, nothing for me." Oriana said with a smile.

"My friends, I present to you, Joan of Arc!'" Greg made a announcement.

The lights were dimmed and the room was dark. Greg pressed a button, and suddenly the screen came alive with a brilliance of light. The music brought the film title into view. Oriana felt the excitement building in Tim's arm. Instantly, she was caught up in the wonders of the film. It was fascinating to see the scenes with Tim playing the king's role! His performance was superb! She was delighted to have him as her boyfriend. She realized that the greatest actor in her life was the man sitting beside her! His eyes were glued to the screen, as she reached over to hold his hand. She was so proud of him!

Returning back to the film, Oriana found herself thrilled with the dynamism of her character and the story line. Like a young girl, watching an idolized movie star on the movie screen, she watched herself with such great performance and acting. Greg pointed out his favorite part of Oriana's act with such enthusiasm and excitement. They seem to be pleased about both performances. The film was ending beautifully! Oriana was amazed at Ellie's talent in directing and she expressed her thoughts with them. After all, she had been a movie star, and this film was her first experience as a director.

The lights came back on the theatre, and everyone was speechless. Even Greg was shocked at how well Ellie had directed the film.

"I can't believe what we just saw! This is definitely a Oscar material movie! Thank you for letting us be a part of it!" Oriana remarked kindly.

"We're so happy to have found you for this film. You are the perfect actor for this movie! Both your performances have added greatly to this film. We are lucky to have you as our best friends as well!" Ellie replied honestly.

"Let's make a toast! To our success!" Greg said, looking at them raising their glass.

Driving home, Tim couldn't wait to talk about his inner thoughts with Oriana.

"What do you think honey?" Oriana asked, starting the conversation.

Tim stayed silent, but instead, he took her hand to his lips and kissed it gently.

"You didn't answer my question honey!" She persisted, looking at him sideways.

"I loved it! What do you think of my acting?" He asked, wanting her honest opinion.

"I think your acting was exceptional! Someday, I'll tell my grand children about you! I will tell them, that you were a great actor and I loved watching the film sitting next to you!" She replied proudly.

• • •

Easter was approaching, and Joan was in distress. She spent, the Palm Sunday in her cell, when the rest of the people attended church. The first stage of her trial, took one month to complete, and she wondered how much more it will take, before it was all over.

The court did not tolerate her sharp remarks, nor her wearing men's clothes! She insisted on wearing them to the trial. It was deeply shocking, to the minds of people that age, that she made all her costumes, with her own two hands in prison. Now, Joan had to be proven guilty!

The law had to find her guilty, to satisfy its English backers. The church had hand in that conspiracy, to burn her, to stamp out an insidious heresy. When she appeared before the ranked assessors, at the trial, she was a deplorable object. Still, she had enough spirit, and common sense, to refuse the services of the church counsel.

"For admonishing me, of my salvation and my faith, I have no intention of departing out from the Lord. Thank you, all the company." She stayed firm on her statement to court.

Later on, Joan heard a article that was written about her. She knew the lies were told by the church, to turn the public against her. It was stated, "At the age of fifteen, she had entered a brothel, and had summoned a certain youth, for breach of promise in whoring. As she grew older, she had become the mistress of a person, and lost everything. That was why she cut her hair short, and had abandoned women's clothes. She didn't care about these ugly lies.

Meanwhile, Joan had become ill again, mostly from trial's

stress and strain. She had fasted to protect herself, but it was over done, sending her near dying. She laid there tirelessly day and night, to take counsel of the church for the salvation of her soul. But, they wasted a good deal of breath on her.

From April 18th to May 9th, Joan was continuously exhorted. In one of her trial day, she told them, "If you were to tear me up, limb from limb under torture, and separate my soul from my body, I would tell you nothing more than I have already. But if I did say anything, I should afterward declare, that you had compelled me to say it by force!"

The court trial was nearly over by May 23rd, and Joan was taken to a room in the castle. One of the judges, addressed her:

"Joan, do not permit yourself to be separated from our Lord, who created you to be a partaker of his glory... it's time, near the end of your trial, to think well over!"

His speech shook her! There was no more to say. She had been found guilty! Could she have been misled? For the past few months, she has been alone in a dark cell, with only three walls surrounding her. She had not seen or heard anything of the outside world. Her king had not lifted a finger to save her, and she had been betrayed and abandoned by her own people.

She broke down, after she heard the verdict. With tears in her eyes, the jailers placed the chains back on her legs. They refused to unlock her, while they shaved her hair. She knew, she was about to die, and was terrified of the fire. She protested to wearing a woman's dress, and wanted to die as a soldier, wearing men's clothing.

• • •

It was a beautiful clear morning in September, when Greg and the movie crew drove back to the Torture Club, to finish a scene. It was the part, where Joan was tortured by her jailers. As the director, Greg considered using a stunt double for that scene, but Oriana persisted to do the scene herself.

In the past couple of weeks, Marcello insisted to accompany his mother to the movie set, so they can spend some time together. Working long hours on the movie scenes, didn't let Oriana see him much.

The Torture Club used to be a privet home, before it was converted. There was a large backyard allowing kids play comfortably. Marcello played catch with other crew member's kids mostly. Sometimes, he sat down on the lawn watching others play. Tim sat next to him on the lawn to keep his company, then tried to make conversation with him.

"When I was your age, my friends and I used to play hide and seek together. Do you know how to play that game?" Tim asked nicely.

"I know how to play that game! I used to play it with my great grand father. Can we play that now?" Marcello asked with excitement.

"OK I will close my eyes, and you try to hide!" Tim said ready to play the game. Looking around the backyard, Marcello walked around a building and saw an open garage door. He hide behind a covered car and waited for Tim to find him. The backyard was in the clear view, so Tim figured to look around the back building. It was a detached single garage, and he noticed the garage door open. Drawing closer to the car, he saw Marcello's shoes behind it.

"I found you!" Tim said quickly. Laughing at loud Marcello tried to come out, but his feet caught into the car cover. Tim went to help him, when he saw a car with paint scratches under it!

Suddenly he recalled Sonia, his previous fiancé, was married to Gary Taylor! Gary is the owner of the Torture Club, and Mary Fawcet's boyfriend! How strange it was that Sonia and Gary used to reside in this property, prior to it's conversion to the Torture Club!

Going over the events in his head, Tim remembered his conversation with the privet detective. He said, "In my conclusion this is a homicide! I have mentioned it in my report that the fatal car accident was caused by another car forcing her car out of the road! The evidence shows that, there are colored markings on the side of her car, as well as the rear. We're sure, that her car was pushed out of control to crash over the bridge purposely! Since we're unable to find the other car involved in that accident, the file remains open and we'll keep searching!"

"I think this is the car!" Tim said at loud, as he checked other markings on the side and the rear bumper of Gary's car.

It was late in the day, Gary Taylor was standing in his home-office looking outside the window. Casually, he watched Marcello and Tim walked away from his garage.

• • •

A few months had gone by since the date of Sonia's terrible car crash. Tim was unsure, whether any of the police detectives were still active on the case. Tim decided to contact the detective previously worked on the case! The phone range on the desk of Detective Shepherd.

"This is Detective Shepherd speaking! Yes ..Who?... Dr. Forist?... Sorry I don't recall!....No news on your ex-fiancé case!.... .Where? Torture Club!?...In Santa Barbara!?... Ok, I'll see you there!" The detective said as he run out of his office.

The case file was picked up on the way, as he hurried with his partner out of the police department. A half-hour later, the detective arrived with a Search Warrant in his hand! He asked retained the information, and had Tim describe what he had witnessed. As a back up and safety of all, there were two other additional police cars accompanied them. Tim pointed out the location of the car, and waited with Marcello by the police car.

Cautiously, the police and the detective approached the garage. Entered inside and pushed the car cover to the side! The sound of the police cars and the commotion in the street, made Gary Taylor go out toward the garage. The police drew their guns and waited, when he walked into his garage!

"Excuse me officer, is there any problem?" Gary asked curiously. He stood next to the car. Obviously, he wasn't comfortable with the situation there.

"Is this your car sir?" Detective Shepherd asked him, ignoring his question.

"Yes it is! What seems to be a problem?" Gary responded, with a shock on his face.

"What is your name?" The Detective asked point blank.

"My name is Dr. Gary Taylor." He responded to the question.

"Are you related to Sonia Taylor?" The Detective asked calmly.

"Yes, she was my ex-wife!" He replied in confusion.

"You are under arrest for homicide of Sonia Taylor! We have a warrant to search the property! Please put your hands up! " The Detective said without any hesitation. Gary was hand cuffed and placed inside a police car quickly.

• • •

Some soft giggles and ghostly whispers woke up Joan from her sleep. A man with rough hands was trying to fondle her body. She opened her eyes in horror, and struggled hard to release her hands held tight above her head. There were two jailers, with a kerosene lamp, standing outside the cell. They seemed to be drunk, dancing around, touching, chattering, and giggling. Their shadows twisted, and writhed on the walls of the cell. One of the jailers leaned in close to kiss her, Joan could hear their heavy breathing, and smell the sour odor of their sweat. She let out a deep breath, and began to shake her chain. One of them reached out, and ran his hand on her breast, and the other, held her feet. The jailer went on top, held up her hand, grabbed her thigh, and raped her. Joan screamed so loud, that filled the cell! The pain was so much, that she could not move! She struggled more to free herself, but felt his penis inside of her! It was a true nightmare, a fountain of blood gushed out of her!

"Oh God! No.......No!" She said in horror, as blood exited her body.

"God...oh...God!" As she began to call on him. Screaming, lashing out, with her hands in chains, wildly, and blindly, she whispered, "I will kill you".

"No!... No!... Stop it!" She said in anguish, when the jailers changed their positions.

She heard something rip! He was tugging on her pants, trying to push it out of the way. Then, he put his entire weight on top of her. Breathing was difficult. Her body was reacting to the shock, and inside she was hurting bad. Tears began to fall from her eyes, when the jailers got up, tightened their trouser, humiliated her, and left the cell.

• • •

On the set of the movie, Greg Mitchell was about to wrap up the day's work. The film was going on schedule, and all the movie shots from the prison was done brilliantly.

"Cut! Cut! That was absolutely great Oriana. Just perfect!" Greg shouted out, as the lights were turned off and the crew started to organize for the next day's movie shooting. The wardrobe woman had already draped Oriana with a towel and Ellie was talking to her about the next scene. Suddenly Mary rushed in!

"What's wrong Mary?" Ellie asked with concern.

"The police just arrested Gary! They suspect Gary had killed his ex-wife!" Mary said innocently in a shock.

"I think you know something about that! Don't you?" Ellie remarked suspiciously.

"Yes I do, but I'm not sure if it's anything! It was a few months ago, when one night Gary came home looked upset! He seemed to be disturbed by something, but didn't want to tell me about it. This happened before we converted the house into a club!" Mary replied to her aunt Ellie calmly.

"So, what do you think happened?" Ellie asked curiously, making Mary think back a little.

"I don't really know! I want to lock up the building, are you done filming?" Mary asked in daze.

"Yes we are, but there is a big scene tomorrow where the English court orders to kill Joan on fire!" Ellie explained the movie scene.

"Aunt Ellie, do you need me on set tomorrow?" Mary asked anxiously.

"No dear! Thanks for everything," Ellie replied, giving her a hug.

The next day on the movie set of the club, a group of reporters approached Ellie. They had a few questions regarding the previous night's police arrest. Ellie answered their questions calmly and honestly. She indicated, that Dr. Taylor's arrest had nothing to do with their film, and would not affect their movie production.

"We're using the club to shoot a few more scene today, but we should be done by tomorrow." Greg explained casually.

Quickly spotting Tim and Marcello on the movie set, the reporters rushed over to get Tim's explanation.

"Please tell us what happened yesterday Dr. Forest!" The reporter asked.

"It all started very innocently, when Marcello and I were playing hide and seek. I discovered the car inside Dr. Taylor's garage accidentally,. The car was covered with a white sheet, away from public's view. It was pure luck, when I checked the car and saw some scratches on the side, rear, and the front of his car! It perfectly corresponded with the description given to me, by Detective Shepard regarding my ex-fiancé's car. The detective believed, that it was a homicide! I contacted the detective, and reported my suspicion on Mr. Taylor's car. It appears that the police have the right man in the custody! I believe, he is the man who murdered my ex-fiancé Sonia! I want to find justice for her! I have to publicly thank Marcello, for accidental discovery of the car. I believe it was the destiny that guided us there!" Tim made his speech, and the news media scattered to break the news.

The next day, the detectives called Tim. He asked to stop by their office to make the report of the incident. Tim was happy to cooperate in any way possible. During Gary Taylor's incarceration, he denied having anything to do with the accident. But when the investigators showed him the crime scene photos, and evidence collected from his car, he made a full confession!

14

Innocent

Early in the morning, May 30, 1431, Joan woke up in sever pain. Her legs were chained to a wooden beam, and her jailers had raped her ruthlessly, the previous night! Two judges, a priest, and a few strong English soldiers, went to Joan's prison cell. One of the judges, read the unanimous decision made against her. She was to be burned, at the stake, within the hour!

"I had holly spirits visiting me again! Through them, God spoke to me! Soon, I shall be with my saints in paradise! In my time of weakness, I had abjured God, and damned my soul to save my body." She told them.

Joan was given a dress to wear, but she tore it off, and put on her own soldier's clothes. More than 10,000 people, stood there to watch her die. She was brought by a cart to the mar-ketplace, where the stake was raised. Once again, Joan felt as if each of her senses were heightened. Only this time, she did not smell the moist freshness of the earth, or hear the singing of the birds. The foul stench of blood, and excrement, assaulted her senses. She could taste the coppery blood in her mouth.

The smell of her death, hung in the air. Her head was shorn and bare, when she was led by English armed escorts, to the awaiting executioner.

Before she was tied to the stake, she knelt and began to pray aloud. She begged God for mercy and forgiveness. Then she shouted, "Ah Rouen, I have great fear, that you will suffer for my death!"

Hastily, the guards took her to the scaffold, and bounded her to the stake. Joan asked for a cross. Someone in the crowd, tied two sticks together for her. He held them up to comfort her, in the last dreadful moments. When the executioner flung oil on the lowest flames, the fire spread out, and smoke rose above. The smell of sculpture hung in the air. Joan was obscured from the sight by the smoke, but the crowd heard her say the last cry, "Jesus!"

It was over! The English executioners, had her ashes scattered, and thrown into the Seine River. She was only 19 years old!

• • •

The final scene of the film was Joan's court sentence. In that scene, the English executioner's were ordered to burn her body on the cross shaped stakes. The fire department had to be present to clear the security and safety measures of the crew. The fire department agreed to stand by during the shooting of the scene.

The actors rehearsed the scenes many times. Oriana believed Greg was a great director and trusted him completely. He made everything look easy. Again, Greg asked Oriana not to do the scene but she persisted to do the scene herself. It was time for Greg to show her a few tricks of the trait!

With a help of a professional stunt person, Oriana learned how to play her role at the fire scene. A rope tied around her body had to be opened up in a short few seconds, and quickly finding her way down the porthole to a hidden ladder going under the deck, before the fire caught up to her. They rehearsed the process over and over again, until she was confident with her acting. It was the most exciting stunt that she had ever done. She had to concentrate on her work and get it done fast!

The fire department suggested the fire scene shooting be done on a old dusty farm house outside Santa Barbara area. For the safety of all crew members, Greg agreed to keep the movie set in a secluded area. The movie crew prepared the scene with a large firewood ring approximately eight feet a round. In the center of the circle, a cruciform was erected. The firewood was placed around the circle to give a look of reality, just as It was done in the real story!

The night before shooting of the scene, Oriana couldn't sleep. She laid still in bed trying hard not to disturb Tim's sleep. Reviewing her steps in her head, out of the fire circle, gave her peace of mind. Covering her face with a soft quilted pink silk sheets, she tried to sleep. Trying different techniques such as counting sheep, or counting numbers backwards didn't work! She was restless and nervous about the fire scene the next day. Somehow, she had to get control of her nerves, otherwise it would turn into a disaster!

The night crawled on. "Sleep!" she told herself, forcing her mind to slow down from thinking too hard, but she remained awake! How frustrating! The anger and extreme helplessness took over her, making her more tense and rigid!

Finally, just before the sun rise she drifted into a shallow sleep. She was awakened in a cold sweat. Her forehead pounded, pulse was racing, and her thighs were sticky. She reached down her legs and felt the moisture there. In an instant she was frozen in horror!

It was 7:00a.m. when Tim woke up. He was shocked to see Oriana wide awake. She struggled to sit up, but quickly he reached over and held her in his arms.

"What's wrong honey? Did you sleep at all last night?" He asked lovingly.

"No honey, I had nightmares!" she said, yawning.

"I'm sorry honey! Let me get you some coffee." he said calmly.

"OK honey, I'm taking a shower to get ready." Oriana replied, thinking that would help her nerves to calm down more.

On the movie set, the crew were busy setting up the stage. Greg was directing the light technicians and cameramen on their location. Everyone was ready in their places. The movie clapper man snapped his board in front of the camera one, the actors heard the word, "Rolling!".

"Action!" Greg shouted out the magic word.

On the deck behind the camera crew, Tim stood watching the scene. He didn't want to miss his girlfriend's fine performance that day. But more than anything, he was worried about her lack of sleep!

As it was done in the real story, the English soldiers brought her to the circle of fire and tied her body to the cross. The fire was set underneath her feet in the center of the circle. As the fire burned more, smoke got darker and thicker. Oriana tried to open the rope from her body in the fire circle, but it took longer time than it was expected! Tim was afraid of the flame reaching her before Oriana had a chance to free herself from it. Luckily, she found her way down the porthole to the hidden ladder, and went under the deck before the fire caught up to her. This was a danger-ous scene and all eyes were glued to the set!

The camera was still rolling on the unfinished flame on the deck. It was following the town's people reaction witnessing Joan's body burning on the cross. A dummy model resembling Oriana, was placed in the center of flame as fire burned it to the ground.

"Cut!" Greg shouted at loud. "That was brilliant Oriana!"

The movie crew who witnessed the scene, admired Oriana's courage and beauty. Her performance was superb! They clapped their hands as the fire department moved to put off the circle's fire.

"You created a masterpiece darling! This was a historical film production done in perfection! It sure deserves an Oscar!" Greg remarked as he got closer to Oriana.

"Bravo darling! Just brilliant!" Ellie said, as she hugged her.

• • •

Finally, the filming of Joan of Arc was successfully complet-ed and production was seized. Making a movie is like having a extended family members, everyone cared about one another and watched out for each other. They were sad to lose their family members, from hair stylist, make-up artist, and assistant production crew, to the actors, director, and producers. They embraced and said goodbye. It was Oriana's charm and Italian personality, that the crew loved the most. She always treated people nicely and respected them. Most of the male crew members loved her gorgeous body, beauty and great mind.

A few days later Ellie organized a party at the hotel. It was for the benefit of the crew members, but mostly for the film's publicity. Ellie had called upon the news media, and reporters to attend as well. Oriana dressed in a white strapless dress, with her boyfriend Tim on her side. He looked handsome in his black suit. As they walked into the party, everyone turned to look at them. The photographers took pictures and they were interviewed.

"Ellie, you look smashingly beautiful tonight!" Oriana remarked as Ellie kissed her.

"I wanted this to be a special party, and to appreciate everyone's hard work." Ellie replied sincerely.

"We are going to miss you. This was a memorable experience for both of us." Tim responded honestly.

"My dearest friends to show our appreciation, Greg and I decided to send you to our villa in Kauai. You deserve to rest after a hectic film shooting. When would you like to go?" Ellie asked with excitement.

"Wow....Thanks darling! I don't know what to say!" Oriana responded happily, looking at Tim for approval.

"Say yes! Let's get you some drinks now" Ellie replied walking to the party's bar.

• • •

The jumbo jet landed at the Kauai Island. It was the last Friday of October, a beautiful sunny day. Tim, Oriana and Marcello arrived to the airport, and the reporters were tipped off about their arrival. A large crowd of journalists, waited impatiently outside the airport gates. Ellie's house manager Roxy, a kind beautiful middle-aged woman, greeted them at the airport with floral leis.

A long black limo was waiting for them outside the airport to take them to a helicopter landing, as It was planned. The limo pulled up close to the helicopter and their luggage were placed on board. During the flight, Roxy was pointing out the famous sights as they flew over the ocean, mountains, and resorts on Kauai Island. It took twenty minuets before the helicopter finally landed on a pad.

Tim had never been so happy in his life before. Being with the most beautiful creature in the world made him feel special. He was so in love with her, and knew she belong to him. Looking back at the past few months, he realized how sad he'd been after Sonia's accident. Oriana was the one who had changed his life for better, and for that he was grateful to her.

At the entrance of the villa, two local ladies in Hawaiian dresses welcomed them with leis. A fruit basket and wine was offered as a gift. Roxy took them on a tour of the house. There were five large bedrooms with the view of the ocean, and five baths. A large living room and dining room combined. The kitchen had the state of the art electronic gadgets, and the backyard had a swimming pool, Jacuzzi, and a tennis court. It was a luxurious house for rich and famous guests.

Finally the day ended, Roxy left with a promise to come back the next day. She offered Marcello to go canoeing around the island. The sunset was brilliant, as they gazed at the horizon. Marcello was tired from the trip, so Oriana tucked him in bed. They sat on the beautiful patio, and drank their wine. It was like being in paradise!

She tip toed in the bedroom and locked the door. Finally they were alone! Tim turned on the music and with one swift move, he pulled her into his arms. His kisses were warm and gentle on her neck, and she was thirsty for his attention and passionate kisses. She stopped him for a moment, and leaned him against the bed's headboard. He did as she desired, like he was hypnotized by her love. She stood up and stripped her clothes off her body one by one, as she danced provocatively with the music. The wine made her feel losing control, and Tim enjoyed watching her nude body in front of him. He took his shirt and pants off, as he watched her every move. Her hands moved slowly from her lips down to her breast. His passion rose higher, as she cupped her breasts in her hands, moving them closer to each other in the center while dancing slowly and moving her hips. Tim enjoyed every movement on the floor and wanted more!

Suddenly, one of her hand moved down lower to her soft stomach and belly button. Within a few seconds, she lowered her hand toward her vagina. Stroking it softly, her finger moved slowly inside as he watched her. She tilted her head back and released a sigh. Her body moved to respond to her newly found pleasure, as he felt more excitement building in his body. He wanted her to continue pleasuring herself, so he waited patiently for the right moment.

Her finger remained inside of her longer, as she took her other hand toward her lips. She sucked on her finger tips, as she reached deeper inside. It was the most exquisite feelings she had ever known! Moving closer to him on the bed, she reached out to him with all her desires! Holding his hard penis in her hand, he drew her closer to him. Kissing her gently on stomach, as he directed his lips lower to where her fingers were! Softly, he placed his warm wet lips on her fingers still inside of her, and urging her fingers out to be quickly replaced by his warm tongue inside her vagina! She stood there frozen, as if she was in a trans! Allowing him to pleasure her with his passion. Taking it all in, as she encountered a out of body experience!

Electric flashes of desire were whipping through her body. She closed her eyes and felt a need to make love to him. Relaxing with his passionate kisses, her legs parted to each side, as she surrendered to him. That was the moment, he had been waiting for! He entered inside of her, as it felt like capturing the highest mountains! Their body were in full synchronized, as she held him closer to match his thrusts! Both consumed with desires, as they reached orgasm together. The small nerves in their body began to spasm, as they quivered like an earthquake after shocks! They were totally drained out of energy and weak lying down next to each other on bed.

From the first moment they met, she had fallen in love with him. He was a great man, a great lover and her true love. "I love you!" Tim said to her, before they fell asleep.

Five days had passed into their vacation on the island. The vacation had affected their relationship and friendship together. They spent quality time visiting the sights, swimming, canoeing, and playing tennis together. One day as they took a shower together, Tim suddenly remembered something! He put on a robe and went to his suitcase. There was a medium size box with a special wrapping paper on it. Oriana was sitting at the make up table, drying her hair. He bent over to kiss her.

"Happy Birthday my love!" He said affectionately.

"Birthday? Oh……Tim!" She said in disbelief.

"How did you know?" she asked playfully.

"That's a secret! Open your present!" he replied, giving her the box.

She unwrapped the box. It was a pearl set of earrings, necklace and bracelets mixed with gold. She was shocked!

"Thank you darling. I love them!" She replied, putting her arms around his neck. She was standing there in nude, when he put the necklace on her.

"I love them even more now!" She remarked excitedly

"They are from China. I bought them when I was living in China. They say it brings good luck!" He replied honestly.

"I love you honey!" She kissed him.

"We're going to have a special celebration for your birthday. Just the three of us." Tim announced.

While getting dressed, she noticed her breasts and nipples were sore and very tender. She realized that she has missed her period, and there hasn't been any bleeding. She was pregnant again!

"Please God, let this baby live! I want to have a family with him! Please don't take that away from me!" She prayed desperately.

One hour later, Oriana went on the patio dressed beautifully. The sun was gentle on her bare shoulders. The ocean looked calm and the weather temperature was just perfect. Tim was with Marcello in the pool, teaching him how to swim.

"Mommy, Mommy look! I can swim now!" the boy yelled out loud. He was able to swim the length of the pool with some help.

Oriana clapped her hand to show her support. Marcello came out of the pool and ran up to her. He had bunch of beautiful tropical flowers grouped together.

"Mommy, this is for you! Happy birthday!" Marcello said innocently. She felt so emotional and burst into tears.

"Honey thank you, I love all your flowers. I have to share some good news with you two! What do you think if mommy brought you a brother or a little sister?" She asked him, looking at their loving eyes.

"Are you saying, that we're going to have a baby?" Tim asked with joy. While Marcello was surprised, looking at both of them with puzzled eyes.

"Yes! I'm pregnant with our baby!" She replied with joy and tears ran down her face. She embraced them both and wouldn't let go.

"I'm going to be a daddy! You are going to be my son Marcello!" Tim said happily, patting the boy on the head.

"You are going to be my Dad? I want a baby girl!" Marcello replied quickly.

The limo approached the house. It was Roxy with two large boxes, a bouquet of beautiful local flowers, and a chocolate cake with candles.

"Happy birthday darling! This morning, I received these two boxes from Ellie and Greg for your birthday. The flowers and the cake are from me." She said nicely.

"You must make a wish, and blow the candles!" Roxy said sweetly as she placed the cake in front of her.

"OK let me close my eyes and make a wish!" Oriana said excitedly. She blew the candles quickly, and began cutting the cake for everyone.

"Honey, aren't you going to open your gifts?" Tim said impatiently.

"Sure, but I like Marcello help me open them." Oriana replied, nodding her head.

Inside, the box she found an emerald gold necklace with matching earrings. Inside the second box, there was a diamond necklace which was custom fitted just for her. She was amazed as how Ellie and Greg would send such a valuable gift for her birthday.

Tim and Marcello went to the beach to swim, leaving Oriana and Roxy alone to talk with each other. Roxy was a great lady, and Oriana was beginning to like her a lot.

"I can feel how much you're in love with him. There is no way to explain why, we fall in love with certain people, but I think you and Tim have something special together!" Roxy said kindly.

"Yes, he is a special man, a very attractive man. I know he is crazy about me, as much as I'm crazy about him!" Oriana said, as she walked Roxy to the door. She hugged her, like she would her own mother.

Suddenly, her cell phone rang and she answered.

"Hello?" Oriana said answering her phone.

"Hello Oriana. This is Loretta!" The caller responded.

"Chow Loretta, is everything OK?" Oriana asked, now speaking Italian.

"No, your mother is in the hospital!" She answered in Italian.

"Your mother asked me to call you, and find out if you are able to come to Naples to see her?" Loretta continued on.

"Ok, tell her I'm coming to see her soon!" Oriana replied, ending the call.

15

The Naples
Goddess

Naples, Italy

THE JUMBO JET DEPARTED Los Angeles Airport to Rome, carrying their passengers on a thirteen hour flight. Sitting in the first class section of the airplane, Tim made sure that Oriana and Marcello were seated comfortably. The passengers sitting in the coach section, were aware that two movie stars were on board. They recognized Oriana from the cover pages of the magazines.

Relaxing on his chair, Tim flipped through pages of Los Angeles Times. Suddenly, he came across a headline which got his full attention! It said, "Dr. Gary Taylor, the owner of celebrity's Torture Club, had been arrested and accused of killing his ex-wife. The prison officials have reported, that Gary was killed in his cell by another prisoner. The police official are investigating the matters."

Oriana noticed a change came over him after reading of the newspaper article! She guessed, it must be related to Gary Taylor! He shook his head in disbelief but was satisfied with the outcome! The justice was served!

A few hours before landing, the airplane went through a thick cloud and there were some turbulence.

"Honey, are you okay?" Tim asked her girlfriend.

"I feel sick a little in my stomach. Let me close my eyes and get some rest." She remarked feeling tired.

Falling into a deep sleep, she woke up by the airplane shaking and rattling, as it began it's descent. She went to the lavatory, touched up her make up, combed her long hair, and returned back to her seat.

Finally, the airplane landed and the doors opened up. Marcello, held his mom's hand as they exited the plane.

"Home again! Naples, Italy!" she said proudly.

Everything about her was interesting. From her slender frame, to her long legs. Her self-assured movement, and perfect physical beauty, she truly stood out among other beautiful woman.

Quickly, Oriana spotted her mother and relatives. They were waving to her and smiling, trying to get her attention.

"Hi Mom!" she called out as she got closer. Gina took Marcello's hand and gave her daughter a hug. Oriana was happy that her mom was out of the hospital and healthy again.

A few things had been circling Oriana's mind lately! This question occupied her mind over again! "What more can I ask for?" As a 25 years young woman she had it all; beauty, good health, perfect figure, great looks, and more wealth than she could handle! This should've been enough to make her feel great, but adding to the list of her blessing were; the most famous international movie star, great son, and live in a dream house in two different continents. She was thankful to have a successful career, and a charming handsome man at her side who loved and cherished her! She was the happiest woman on earth! Still, there were two more things that she could ask for, and wanted the most! Getting married to the love of her life Tim, and to give birth to a healthy little bundle of joy! That would make it the most complete and perfect life!

Once inside the large limo, Gina held Marcello closely on her lap and asked her something in Italian! She didn't want Tim to know about their privet conversation!

"How long have you been pregnant?" Gina asked point blank.

"Around two months Mom!" She answered, while holding Tim's hand.

"Are you wanting to keep the baby?" Gina said, showing great concern for her.

"Yes mom don't worry! It's different this time!" Oriana said, patting her mom's lap.

"Is he your future husband?" Gina asked, making sure there are marriage plans in the future.

"Yes mom he is!" Oriana said with a big smile on her face.

"I'm happy for both of you!" Gina said in Italian.

Oriana translated it into English, making everyone to smile.

It was a exhausting week for Tim, he had to get adjusted to the new time zone. Mostly he read newspapers and magazine articles. A few times, Oriana woke up during the night and didn't find him in bed. She put her robe on and went down the stairs to the living room. There he was sitting on the couch reading a newspaper. He noticed her walk in, pushing his newspaper to the side, he made room for her to sit down on his lap.

"You seem restless darling! I'm sure you miss working and staying busy. I was talking to Loretta yesterday, she said they can use some help at the studio! Would you like to manage the studio for a little while?" She asked her sweetheart.

"I'm sure they are managing fine. Have they been profitable?" Tim asked with interest.

"They are doing ok but not profitable! My mom doesn't want me to manage the studio specially in this condition..." Oriana said honestly.

"Honey, I don't know anything about managing a movie studio and..." Tim said with humor.

34444334

"Darling you were an actor in a film, I'm sure you know how to manage an office?" She asked casually.

"Yes I did, but I had a great teacher like you. didn't I?" Tim replied, trying to compliment her.

"You wouldn't be alone darling, Loretta and I would be right beside you. It's a team effort!" She remarked trying to make her point.

"Yes, but I don't know anything about directing and…" Tim said with frustration.

"Don't worry honey. You can ask our friends, Ellie and Greg when you have any questions. Please try it for me honey!" She asked, trying to persuade him.

"OK honey!" He responded, willing to cooperate.

"Thanks honey. We could go to the studio after our breakfast." She replied happily.

Loretta was expecting their arrival at the studio. Oriana made a call earlier to let her know about a emergency meeting with the studio executives. Loretta was the "go to person" in the company, and was considered the right hand person to her grandfather's business. A sixty five year old respected woman, who worked hard at the office and was trusted at the studio by the family. She was aware about Oriana's feelings toward her boyfriend Tim.

The limo driver opened the door quickly and helped Oriana out of the car. She was wearing a beautiful summer dress, trying to conceal her pregnancy. They walked up the stairs slowly to Gina's office. Loretta welcomed them and guided them to the conference room. A few other executives were waiting for their arrival. They spoke English when Tim was introduced to them.

Since Oriana's last visit, Loretta had rearranged the office furniture but kept her grandfather's office intact. His hand painted large picture was hanging in the conference room's wall. Oriana and her mother were pleased with the new office look. The conference room's door closed behind them, once everyone entered and were seated.

Loretta thanked everyone coming to the meeting, and Oriana began talking about her plans. Everyone was clear that Tim would begin helping Loretta manage the studio by bringing new ideas to the table, from the American business perspective point. She was hopeful that it would ultimately boost the production of their existing business. The meeting was productive for all parties, specially when Loretta found out about Oriana's pregnancy.

• • •

At the end of November, Ellie Mitchell informed the movie news media, that Joan of Arc was about to be released in the theaters. Her plans were to allow the movie goers watch the film for few weeks, making it eligible for the best film nomination for best actor and director in the Oscars. She wished to win the Oscars by end of February.

It was the biggest news in the movie industry where everyone had heard about the film for so long, and were waiting to finally see it! The news spread very fast, like the wild flower. The media requested to interview Oriana about the movie. She agreed to do a press conference after she returned to Hollywood.

The Naples's media began to show even more interest with Oriana visiting Italy. They asked to interview Oriana, who played the role of "Joan of Arc", getting information about the production and distribution of the movie there. She agreed to do a informal press conference at her studio. The news reporters were anxious to see her, and take photos from every angel. Oriana answered each question thoughtfully. Some questions were personal asking about her relationship with Tim.

"He is a great man and I love him. We hope to get married soon after the Oscars. He recently accepted to help with the management of our studio!" she responded to the reporters, and turned to look at him with loving eyes. He kissed her and The photographers went wild to take a picture of them.

"What do you think about distribution of 'Joan of Arc' in Europe?" The reporter asked impatiently.

"It's planned for the distribution of the film in Europe after the Oscars. We understand that the Europeans could relate to the film, since it was a true story of "Joan of Arc". When that happens, our ticket sales would go sky high!" she responded beautifully.

"Miss Rousliny, is there any chance that you would make another film together?" The reporter asked curiously.

"I can't answer that! But if by chance, we obtain the perfect screen play right for us, sure that might be a good chance that we do that project together again!" she replied politely.

Some of the questions were getting too personal, and it was time to end it. "Thank you everyone for coming." Tim interrupted nicely, guiding her down the stairs.

The Hollywood entertainment news showed the footage of Oriana's news conference in Naples, Italy. Within the first week after showing of Joan of Arc movie at the theatre, the rating in the box office had gone up to number one on the chart. The ticket sales were shooting to the roof! To maximize on their profit, some movie theaters decided to show the film in two to three screens in their theater! Everyone were sure that this movie would win Oscar!

The Italian news media were covering the story on the film in Hollywood as often as they could. Joan of Arc the movie was favored among other movie. It was reported that the film had been in the number one position for the past three weeks! The Italian TV reporter conducted interviews with ordinary people in Naples, asking if they were interested to see the movie there. Most people indicated, that they couldn't hardly wait to see the film!

As the new manager of the studio, Tim decided to talk to Ellie Mitchell in Hollywood about the early release of "Joan of Arc" in Europe. She agreed that the timing was great. With Loretta's help, they planned to show the premier of the film at a upcoming Film Festival there. A famous movie theater in Naples was chosen for that purpose alone.

A advertising campaign team were chosen to carry out the task, at the Naples's studio. It was a smart move to pre-sale the tickets. Within hours, they were sold out! The demand to see the film was more than they anticipated! This was a huge success! Oriana was so happy and proud about his decision making. He had a great common sense and business mind, similar to her grandfather! Tim was very loving and extremely protective of her. His heart was filled with joy as she neared her last tri-master of pregnancy.

Early February was planned for their wedding. It was first time marriage for both of them, and they wanted it to be special. She wore a simple white dress, with beautiful flowers on her hair. Tim had chosen a lightweight white suit for the occasion. There were two hundred guests hand picked by both of them to attend the wedding ceremony. From Hollywood, Ellie and Greg flew to Italy to witness this happy event. Among the guests were their families, friends, and local celebrities.

"We have gathered here, to witness this man and woman join into a happy matrimony......... ," The minister began the ceremony.

Oriana had memorized the words she intended to say, but somehow they were scrambled around her mind like sparkling marbles, sending off starbursts of happiness as they jostled from her soul.

"Do you, Oriana Rousliny, take Tim Forist to be your lawful wedded husband?" Minister asked, as he waited for her response.

"I do!" she replied, with a big smile.

"Do you, Tim Forist, take Oriana Rousliny to be your lawful wedded wife?" The minister asked turning toward Tim.

"I do!" He replied, looking at Oriana with tears in his eyes.

His heart was filled with pride and joy. The Lord had blessed him with such a beautiful woman, a great step son, and a baby soon. What more can he ask for! It's time to march toward more greatness!

"Now, with the power vested in me, I pronounce you husband and wife! You may kiss the bride!" The minister remarked with excitement in his voice.

He reached out to take her hand. With one quick move, he rolled her into his arms and sealed her lips with a kiss. That provoked a rising storm of cheers and whistles from friends. The guests clapped their hands, as he picked her off the ground and carried her down the isle. Oriana felt safe being cradled against the warmth and strength of his vast chest. This was such a incredible moment and happiest time of her life!

• • •

On the morning of February 26th in Naples, Italy, Oriana was awakened suddenly! Looking at the clock on the table, it was 8:30am, and Tim had already gone to work.

"Oh God!" She said, feeling pain.

"Marcello? She called out.

Minutes later, Marcello walked into her bedroom rubbing his eyes. She felt water running down her legs. Her night gown was socking wet and she was terrified!

"Marcello sweetheart, can you get grandma for me!" She said desperately, feeling her labor pains.

Every TV station in Hollywood was waiting for the Oscar celebrations. There were live interviews with movie stars on the red carpet, and breaking news. The searchlights aimed at the sky, were crisscrossed against the blackness of the sky. All movie fans in the bleacher's seats took pictures of their favorite movie stars arriving and posing for photographers. The nominees for the best films, male actor, female actress, and best director were announced previously before Oscars night. The film Joan Of Arc was already considered among one of the best movies in the film category.

The movie stars presenting the Oscars arrived by their limousines. They walked on the red carpet and posed for the photographers. Everyone were seated and waiting eagerly to start the Oscar ceremonies.

"Here we go!" Greg said, adjusting his black bow tie.

"Honey, this is the moment that we've been waiting for!" She remarked with hope, as they walked the carpet to the auditorium.

Ellie prepared herself for what tonight's event would bring to them. She took out her compact powder, and checked her face in the mirror for the last time. She looked perfect and flawless. Everyone seemed to be quiet, but eager to know who would win the Oscar tonight!

It meant so much for Ellie winning the Oscar for the best film and director's nomination. She would finally achieve her lifetime desire to be a director in Hollywood. She was considered to be the brightest and the most beautiful movie star, but being nominated for the best director would be her ultimate wish!

"Ready darling?" Greg asked, gently squeezing her hand.

"I'm ready for the outcome, whatever that may be honey!" she replied with a brilliant smile.

In the hospital delivery room, Dr. Ben Ferman was preparing to deliver the most famous baby in Naples, Italy. He was chosen by Oriana and Tim to be their pediatric doctor. He was scrubbing his hands before he entered into the delivery room. Her husband Tim was standing there coaching her with breathing techniques to keep her calmed down. She was being monitored by nurse Jessica, to report any abnormalities on baby's heartbeat. Outside the hospital, a TV reporter broke the news. He was broadcasting live for the local and international news.

"Hi this is Chelo, reporting to you from general hospital in Naples, Italy. A few hours ago, Oriana Rousliny, our famous Italian movie star and the Oscar nominee for the best actress on Joan Of Arc film, was brought into this hospital to deliver her baby. We understand, she is expected to give birth soon! This is her second child, but her first nomination to win the Oscar tonight! The movie is expected to win for the best film, actor, and director. We are waiting for Hollywood to announce the winners in the next few hours! We wish them the best! I will be reporting back to you with more news later!"

Back to Hollywood, CA, at the Oscar's ceremony two movie stars were making the announcement. "Here are the Oscar nominees for the best film! ....And the winner is, "Joan of Arc!" Ellie and Greg were so excited! With tears in their eyes, together walked on the stage to accept the Oscar! They thanked the movie crew and their movie stars for their hard work. A tense audience waited to hear the next category, the nominees for the best Director! "..........And the winners are, "Ellie and Greg Mitchell!" The audience clapped, supporting the winners while Ellie held on to Greg's arms walking on the stage together to receive their Oscar. Ellie was overwhelmed and speechless! Greg Mitchell took the leadership in thanking the movie crew, Oriana, and his wife for letting him co-direct this magnificent film, and write the script! They hugged each other happily and thanked the Academy.

Back to Naples, Italy. Inside the delivery room, Dr. Ben Ferman and his nurse Jessica were monitoring the progress of Oriana's baby. Due to severity of her labor pains, the epidural injection was administered. The injection helped reduce the labor pains, but prolonged the duration of the delivery time! Outside the hospital, the reporters were eager to hear the good news!

"Hi this is Chelo reporting from the general hospital. We are following up with our story about Oriana Rousliny's baby delivery. Unfortunately, as of now there are no news! But we were told a moment ago, that Hollywood has announced "Joan of Arc" has won the Oscar for best film category as well as the best director's nomination! We take this opportunity to congratulate them, and continue waiting for the baby's delivery announcement. Please stay tuned for more follow up news!"

"Honey push! You are almost there!" Tim said trying to encourage his wife further along. Nurse Jessica was helping him in between the push time, while Dr. Ben was prepared to receive the baby.

"Come on Oriana, you can do this! Push!" Dr. Ben asked her again, getting the push time closer and closer together.

Oriana squeezed and pushed harder, while her hand clinched into her husband's arm. Sweat was running down her forehead and face, clearly she was tired of fifteen hours of labor pain! She wanted to get some rest.

"You are so close! Don't you want to see your baby's face? Don't you want to know if it's a boy or a girl?" Nurse Jessica enticed Oriana to keep pushing.

"I can see the baby's head now! Push a little slowly! Stop when I tell you to!" Dr. Ben Ferman said cautiously.

Back to Hollywood, the most important category for the best female actress was being announced on the stage! Everyone were nervous and sitting at the edge of their seat. "..........And the winner is, Oriana Rousliny for the best actress in "Joan of Arc".

The fans went wild clapping and cheering for her. Ellie and Greg Mitchell were extremely excited for her as well. Knowing she was giving birth at that moment in the hospital, in Naples, Ellie went on the stage to accept the award on her behalf and thank the academy for it! The news media covered the story moment by moment.

"Hi this is Chelo reporting from the general hospital in Naples. This is our second follow up to our story on Oriana Rousliny. We have a important news to share with you! I was just informed that, Oriana Rousliny has given birth to a baby girl! Both the mother and the baby are doing well. We want to congratulate her and her husband Tim Forist on their new bundle of joy! In addition, during her child birth, the Academy has announced the winner in the best female actor category! Oriana Rousliny has won the Oscar! This is unbelievable and extraordinary! Now, she is the best international movie star! Congratulations Oriana!" Please wait everyone! I believe Mr. Forist is making an announcement.

"Thank you everyone! We have two great news to share with you! First, we are blessed and happy to announce our new baby's arrival! It's a Girl! My wife and the baby are doing fine. We have named her Joana! Second, we are excited and honored to receive the Oscar for the best female actor! We knew from the beginning, that there would be a good chance for the film to win the Oscar, but didn't expect for Oriana to win the best actress nomination!" Tim made the public announcement while Oriana and Marcello watched on the television. Her tears of joy began to fall down her cheeks.

Tim returned to the hospital room to be with his wife and new baby. He hugged Marcello and kissed him on the forehead. He was happy to have a baby sister now, and could not wait to get home to hold her. Tim sat on the bed next to his wife and held her hand into his. Looking deeply into her eyes he said, "You are my love and my life! I want to love you and do for you, all that love entails. I want your happiness as much as I want my own, if not more, and this desire will never go away as long as I'm with you! I Love you with all my heart sweetheart!"

About the Author

COL. MAHMOUD IRANPANAH WAS born in May of 1927 in Iran. After finishing high school, he graduated from the Police Service Academy in Tehran. He retired as colonel in 1975, after twenty-six years of service, on the police force. In 1979, while his three children were studying in Los Angeles, CA, he and his wife joined them in United States. He began pursuing his passion in writing.

His passion for writing began at early age. He kept a journal of his daily life, and wrote about different subjects which interested him. As a novelist, he admires the writing style of the well-known French writer, Alexander Dumas. Up to this date, Mahmoud has written over 5,600 pages, and has published over 12 books.

Col. Iranpanah is the first Iranian writer who incorporates sexual and sensual ideas, into his novels cleverly. It's very seldom, that an Iranian writer dares to write about the erotic and sexual fantasies of a character, into his novels.

Mahmoud has received the highest honor, for his last book, from former Empress of Iran, Queen Farah Pahlavi.

List of Books:

The following are, a list of books written up to this date: The Memories of a Police Officer, Three Musketeers in Iran Blood, Twenty Years After, The Wrestler, The Pretty Girl, The Destiny Plays, The Hostage of Nojeh, The Golden Head Soccer Player, Body and Soul, God, Devil, and Ayatollahs.

In addition, the library of Congress in Washington, DC, has obtained, cataloged and made accessible to the public, all the author's published books.

As much as Col. Mahmoud Iranpanah loves being a writer, he also enjoys sport. From an early age, he has participated in all kinds of sport; such as soccer, tennis, volleyball, swimming, and diving.

At age 75, he has participated in the Senior Olympic Games, in Los Angeles, CA. He won the single, double, and mixed-double tennis categories, between 2003, 2005, and 2007. Also, he has received Gold, and Silver medals for swimming, in the freestyle competition, (50, 100, and 200 meter).

At age 83, Mr. Iranpanah is one of the most successful Iranian writers, who has published all his books in Farsi, but he is extremely proud to present to you, his only book, "Joan of Arc", written and published in English.

Made in the USA
Las Vegas, NV
15 December 2020

13461761R00120